"I'm thinking you
down there and I
known what hap

"Thea." He said her name so softly she might have thought the tender missive was nothing more than a breeze sighing through the treetops.

The sun bearing down on them was hot and relentless, but Thea felt a little shiver go through her. It hit her anew how much she'd missed that tender glint in his eyes as their gazes locked. How much she'd missed his husky whispers in the dark. The glide of his hand along her bare skin, the tease of his lips and tongue against her mouth. The way he had held her afterward as if he never wanted to let her go. But he had let her go and she'd done nothing to stop him.

She drew a shaky breath. "Don't ever do that to me again."

"Get caught in a whirlpool? I'll do my best."

She scowled at him. "Don't make light. You know what I mean."

"I'm fine, Thea." He seemed on the verge of saying something else, but he held back. Maybe he thought she wanted his restraint. She did, didn't she? They were in a precarious situation. Adrenaline and attraction could be a dangerous combination. Throw in unresolved issues and they were asking for trouble.

LITTLE GIRL GONE

—

Amanda Stevens

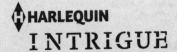

HARLEQUIN

INTRIGUE

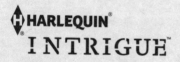

ISBN-13: 978-1-335-48935-7

Little Girl Gone

Recycling programs for this product may not exist in your area.

Harlequin Enterprises ULC
22 Adelaide St. West, 41st Floor
Toronto, Ontario M5H 4E3, Canada
www.Harlequin.com

Printed in U.S.A.

Amanda Stevens is an award-winning author of over fifty novels, including the modern gothic series The Graveyard Queen. Her books have been described as eerie and atmospheric, and "a new take on the classic ghost story." Born and raised in the rural South, she now resides in Houston, Texas, where she enjoys binge-watching, bike riding and the occasional margarita.

Books by Amanda Stevens

Harlequin Intrigue

A Procedural Crime Story

Little Girl Gone

An Echo Lake Novel

Without a Trace
A Desperate Search
Someone Is Watching

Twilight's Children

Criminal Behavior
Incriminating Evidence
Killer Investigation
Pine Lake
Whispering Springs
Bishop's Rock (ebook novella)

MIRA

The Graveyard Queen

The Restorer
The Kingdom
The Prophet
The Visitor
The Sinner
The Awakening

Visit the Author Profile page at Harlequin.com.

CAST OF CHARACTERS

Thea Lamb—Returning to her hometown to search for a missing child, Special Agent Lamb must confront her old suspicions regarding her twin's disappearance...and somehow make peace with the man who left her behind.

Jacob Stillwell—Accepting a promotion took him from the woman he loved. Now the perilous search for another abducted child—and the monster that took her—has brought them together again.

Reggie Lamb—Twenty-eight years after her daughter disappeared, another child has been taken through the same bedroom window.

Kylie Buchanan—The four-year-old disappeared from Reggie Lamb's house, seemingly without a trace.

Taryn Buchanan—How far would a desperate mother go to protect her child?

Russ Buchanan—Cold and calculating, he vowed revenge the day Taryn left with their child.

Grace Bowden—A doll found floating in an underground pool came from her antique doll store.

Chapter One

The faded blue sedan had seen better days. So had the driver, a raw-boned, dauntless woman named Reggie Lamb. Her eyes squinted as she scanned the arriving passengers at Tallahassee International Airport. The sun and her past had carved deep crevices in her leathered complexion and the once blond curls had turned to wiry gray ringlets. She was only forty-nine, but looked at least a decade older.

Watching from afar, Thea Lamb chided herself for the unkind assessment. She wasn't there to find fault with her mother. Another child had gone missing in Black Creek, Florida, and Thea had come down from DC to offer whatever assistance might be needed.

Black Creek.

The very name of her hometown seemed synonymous with the brooding landscape along sections of the Florida-Georgia border, an area far more Deep South than any other part of the Sunshine state. Backwoods was a more apt description in Thea's book. Acres and acres of thick, verdant forest shrouding an underground labyrinth of caverns and springs. A place where screams went unheard and bones could stay hidden forever.

The phantom perfume of moss and mud seeped into Thea's senses until she drew a sharp breath and let the very real odor of exhaust flush away the smell of her nightmares.

Twenty-eight years ago, the first child to go missing had been her twin sister, Maya. She'd been taken from the bedroom where Thea lay sleeping. Even now, dark images floated at the back of her mind when she thought of that night. She had to remind herself that she was a grown woman, a federal agent no longer susceptible to the night terrors of her youth or to the whispers that had once permeated her hometown. But some fears never really went away. Some doubts never truly died.

She'd come down here with the best of intentions, but the past had hovered like a storm cloud ever since she'd boarded her flight. She couldn't help worrying that nothing good would come from a reunion with her mother. The years of estrangement stretched like ten miles of bad road as Thea slung her backpack over one shoulder and wheeled her carry-on out to the curb.

The sedan rattled to a stop and Reggie jumped out to help with the luggage. She was dressed in the typical Floridian uniform of shorts, tank top and flip-flops. Despite her scrawny frame, she hoisted the bulging carry-on into the trunk as if it weighed no more than a handbag. Then she checked the airport traffic before shifting her wary blue gaze to Thea.

"I'm glad you came." She made no move to embrace her daughter and Thea was glad for that.

Heat rose from the pavement, activating perspiration along her backbone as she tried to sound normal. "How are you holding up, Reggie?"

The rasp in her mother's voice deepened. "So it's Reggie now, is it?"

"It has been since I was ten years old. Or had you forgotten?"

"I always preferred Mama."

"It never seemed to suit you," Thea said without thinking.

Something flitted across Reggie's suntanned face. Pain? Regret?

Her mouth tightened, emphasizing the harsh lines. "I guess I can't blame you for feeling that way. I did the best I could, but that's not much of an excuse, is it?"

Something fluttered in the pit of Thea's stomach. Pain? Regret?

This was so much more difficult than she'd anticipated. Her feelings for Reggie were darkly complex, a messy patchwork of anger and resentment stitched together with lingering doubts. Regardless of what else lay between them, Reggie was still her mother, the woman who'd worked double shifts at the local diner to put food on the table and keep a roof over their heads. The woman who'd doctored Thea's skinned knees and sent bullies sniveling home to their mamas when their cruelty had made her cry.

She took a deep breath. "I didn't come here to dredge up the past."

"No help for that, given what's happened," Reggie stated flatly. "Another child has disappeared from my home. Considering my history, you can imagine what the cops are thinking and the neighbors are saying. Half of them already have me on my way to prison."

Thea didn't have to imagine anything. She'd only been four when her sister was taken, but she'd lived in the shadow of Maya's abduction until she'd left home for college at seventeen. She wished she could say she'd learned to ignore the malicious gossip but, truth be told, she'd never been as strong-willed as Reggie. The taunts had always gotten under her skin. *Your mama murdered your twin sister. How do you sleep in the same house with that monster? Ever wonder if you were the one she meant to kill?*

"Is it as bad as it was before?" Thea asked.

"Bad enough." Reggie rubbed the inside of her elbow. "I didn't stay at the house last night, but I ran by there this morning to get some fresh clothes before I went to work—"

"Wait a minute," Thea cut in. "You worked this morning?"

"Why wouldn't I? The town's flooded with state troopers and volunteers, and the diner's shorthanded. Somebody's got to pitch in and help feed them."

"Yes, of course. I just thought under the circumstances…never mind. So you went by the house…?"

Reggie's expression remained stoic but her eyes glittered angrily. "Somebody had spray-painted *murderer* across the side of my porch."

"I'm sorry."

"It is what it is. I tried to scrub it off, but you can still see the outline. Figured you should know what you're walking into."

She nodded, avoiding her mother's gaze. Reggie was still tough as nails on the outside, but Thea had never thought of her as vulnerable until now. With an effort, she swallowed past an unexpected knot in her throat. "I'm still not clear on how Taryn Buchanan and her daughter came to be staying with you in the first place."

"It's a long story. I'll explain everything on the way home, but right now we need to get moving. We're holding up the line."

As if to punctuate her point, a shiny black pickup with tinted windows inched forward impatiently.

Reggie glared at the driver before turning back to Thea. "Get in."

Thea dropped the backpack in the trunk, but kept the cross-body bag containing her SIG-Sauer 9 mm and FBI credentials over her shoulder. She climbed into the passenger seat while Reggie went around and got in behind the wheel. The interior of the car wasn't in much better shape than the outside. The upholstery was worn through in places, and there was a hole in the dash where the radio had been removed. But the motor caught smoothly when Reggie turned the key in the ignition. That wasn't surprising. She'd always been a whiz with engines. Had to be, since there'd never been any money for mechanics.

She was good with engines, but not so much air conditioners, Thea thought as she twisted up her long hair and pinned it in the back. She couldn't remember a time when any of Reggie's old beaters had had working AC. She peeled off her jacket and placed it on the bench seat with her bag.

Reggie gave her a sidelong glance before easing away from the curb. "You always dress like that? Like you're going to a funeral? Girl, you'll melt in this heat."

Thea tried not to bristle at the critique. "I dress for the job, not the weather. People tend to be more cooperative if they're even slightly intimidated by a professional appearance."

"But you're not on the job," Reggie pointed out. "You said you were taking some personal days. So who are you trying to intimidate?"

"No one. I'm here to offer moral support and any other help that may be needed."

Reggie braked suddenly to allow the pickup to whip around her. Muttering under her breath, she double-checked the rearview mirror as she merged with the line of cars exiting the terminal.

"Somebody's in a hurry," Thea said.

"Looks to be," Reggie agreed. "People drive like idiots these days."

"I'm surprised you didn't flip him off. I admire your restraint."

Reggie flashed her a look. "I don't do that sort of thing anymore. I don't do a lot of things I use to. You'd know that if you ever came to see me."

Thea tamped down her irritation. "I'm here now, aren't I?"

"Yes, and I'm grateful for that. God knows I need all the moral support I can get. But let's not kid ourselves as to the real reason you came, *Althea*."

No one had called her that in years. Thea frowned as she dug out her sunglasses. "I'll bite," she said as she slipped on the Wayfarers. "Why am I here?"

"Be honest," Reggie said. "You think Kylie's disappearance is somehow connected to Maya's, don't you?"

"Maya was taken nearly thirty years ago. The likelihood of a connection after all this time is slim."

"Both girls disappeared from my home through the same bedroom window. You're telling me that's a coincidence?"

"No, not a coincidence," Thea said. "It's possible Kylie Buchanan's kidnapper mimicked Maya's abduction to disguise his or her true motive."

Reggie chewed her lip in contemplation, her gaze trained on the road. Traffic was bumper-to-bumper leaving the airport. "The FBI profiler said something similar. She and the other Feds swooped in fast this time. A bunch of SUVs arrived in town just a couple hours after the local cops called for assistance."

"That's good. The sooner CARD hits the ground running, the greater the chances of a positive resolution," Thea said, referring to the FBI's elite Child Abduction Rapid Deployment team. "There's nothing anyone can say that will offer much comfort to Taryn Buchanan at the moment, but you should both know the people out there looking for her little girl are the best of the best. Every agent on that team has years of experience and expertise working crimes against children cases. They have a nearly ninety percent success rate in identifying and apprehending child abductors."

"What about their success rate in bringing children

home safely?" Fear crept into Reggie's voice. "It's been well over twenty-four hours since Kylie went missing. We both know what that means."

"Try not to get hung up on the timeline," Thea advised. "Every case is different." But she knew better than most that nonparental abductions rarely turned out well, especially when the child was a tender age. "Who's the agent in charge?"

"I have his information somewhere." Reggie patted her shorts pocket and withdrew a business card. "Here. A guy named Stillwell."

Thea's heart thudded as she glanced at the card. Special Agent Jacob Stillwell. *Jake.* She'd known their paths would likely cross when she'd made the decision to come down here. He headed the southeast CARD team that worked out of the Jacksonville field office. Stood to reason he'd be sent to Black Creek. Thea told herself she could handle a face-to-face. Whatever they'd once shared had been over for a long time. Jake Stillwell was just a guy she used to know. A colleague with benefits who'd packed his bags and left town with barely a backward glance.

At least, that was the way Thea had regarded his departure at the time. In retrospect, everything about their relationship had been so much more complicated than either had wanted to concede. They'd gone into it with their eyes wide open—or so they'd told themselves. The job would always come first. No guilt. No resentment. No having to justify long hours or making hard choices. When it ended, it ended.

What a crock. After four years, the cavalier way he'd

told her about his transfer still stung, but it would be a cold day in hell before Thea ever admitted it aloud.

She placed the card facedown on the seat and turned to stare out the side window.

"Do you know him?" Reggie asked.

Thea answered in a careful monotone. "Agent Stillwell has an excellent reputation."

"That's not what I mean. Do you know him personally?"

"Why does it matter?"

"I'm just curious. He seems to know you. He asked about you…how you're doing, that sort of thing. I couldn't tell him much seeing as how I don't know the first thing about your life in DC. I don't even know what it is you do all day."

"Mostly, I stare at a computer screen." Thea's fingers curled around the edge of the seat. "As for Agent Stillwell, I'm sure he was just trying to be polite."

"Maybe. But there was something about the way he said your name." Reggie shrugged. "Then again, maybe I imagined his interest."

Thea wasn't about to get into the details of her personal life with her mother. She and Reggie had come to an agreement years ago about staying out of one another's private affairs. But she feared her silence would reveal far more about her feelings than she intended. Reggie was nobody's fool. If Thea didn't give her something, she might end up making an embarrassing assumption in front of Jake. "We worked together a few years back. We were partners for a time."

"What happened?"

Thea adjusted her sunglasses as she gave her mother a frustrated glance. "Nothing happened. He was promoted and transferred to the Jacksonville field office. I stayed in DC."

"Ah," Reggie murmured. "Now I get it."

"What do you get?" Thea demanded.

Her mother shot her a meaningful glance. "I'm guessing his promotion rubbed you the wrong way. You were always crazy competitive, even as a kid. With your classmates, with your sister. Even with me."

Thea swung around. "That's not true. I worked hard to get your attention, but never at Maya's expense."

Reggie looked stricken. Then a mask dropped as her shoulders stiffened. "I'm sorry. I shouldn't have said what I did. You and Maya were always so close. I couldn't punish one of you without the other lighting into me. You were each other's fiercest defender."

Thea winced. "Some defender I turned out to be."

"You were four years old. What happened to Maya wasn't your fault. It wasn't anyone's fault except for the person who took her, though plenty of folks around here still blame me. They think I was the kind of mother who would murder her own child and bury her body in the woods." She gave Thea a long scrutiny. "Maybe you think that, too. Maybe that's why you don't come down here anymore."

JAKE STILLWELL CLIMBED out of the SUV and stood for a moment, letting his gaze roam over the rows of dated brick ranches. The façade color varied, but the houses all had the same carports and concrete porches with scrolled metal posts. None had been updated, but some had been better maintained than others.

The quiet neighborhood was located less than a quarter mile from the center of Black Creek, technically within the town limits, but the mature trees and outbuildings gave the area a rural ambience. A thick canopy of oak leaves hung over the sidewalks, casting deep shadows onto the street.

Under normal circumstances, Jake would have welcomed a respite from the relentless heat, but when he took in the shrouded yards and encroaching woods, all he saw were hiding places. All he could think was how easily someone could move through the neighborhood without being seen.

"Hey! Can I help you with something?"

Jake turned to see the neighbor from across the street ambling down his gravel driveway with a bluetick at his side. The man looked to be nearing sixty, tall and lanky, with grayish-blond hair thinning at the top. He wore a pair of stained cargo shorts and a dingy white T-shirt with a sailfish on the front. The coonhound looked elderly and lethargic, his hunting days long behind him.

"If you're looking for Reggie, she's not home," he informed Jake. "I saw her over there earlier, but that was hours ago. You might try the diner."

"I'm not here to see Reggie."

The man paused at the end of the drive to take a long swig from the insulated mug he carried. His relaxed manner belied the suspicious glint in his eyes. He lowered the tumbler and wiped his mouth with the back of his hand. "Then what's your business here, if you don't mind my asking?"

Good question. Jake wouldn't be able to explain his compulsion even if he were inclined to try. He had come back to Reggie Lamb's house because he'd had to. As simple and as complicated as that. "I'm Agent Stillwell with the FBI."

"FBI, huh?" The man leaned an arm against his rickety mailbox. "I figured you were a cop of some kind, but I wouldn't be much of a neighbor if I didn't ask to see some ID."

Jake took out his credentials and held them up so the man could see the gold badge from across the street.

He squinted in Jake's direction, then crossed the street, flip-flops slapping against the pavement. He called to his companion, who moseyed after him. Jake waited beside his SUV for the languid pair to approach. The man scrutinized Jake's photograph and then reached down to give the dog a reassuring scratch behind a floppy ear. The hound took that as his cue to find a shady spot to stretch out, chin on paws, and wait patiently.

"Sorry for being such a pain in the rear," the man said in a friendlier tone. "Can't be too careful after everything that's happened."

"I agree. It's good that you look out for your neighbors." Jake put away his credentials, his gaze still on the stranger. "I didn't catch your name."

"Lyle Crowder. That's my place over yonder, but you probably already figured that out." He glanced over his shoulder, cocking his head with a frown. "Do you hear that?"

"Hear what?"

He turned back to Jake. "Exactly my point. Yesterday, the police were all over the neighborhood, knocking on doors, searching garages and storage sheds, and today it's like a ghost town around here. Even the helicopter I saw circling earlier is gone." His shoulders hunched as if a cold wind blew down his neck. "Did you find the little girl? Is that why you're here? You came to tell Reggie and her mother in person?"

"Kylie Buchanan hasn't been found," Jake said. "As I understand it, no one is staying here at the moment. The lack of activity in the neighborhood is due to the fact we've expanded the search into other areas. We're trying to cover as much territory as we can in a short amount of time."

Lyle nodded, his eyes dark and knowing. "Lots of woods around here. Lots of lakes and creeks."

"The terrain is challenging," Jake agreed.

"I've been thinking about that old cave on Douglas McNally's property. It's not far from here. A couple of miles through them woods." He nodded toward the back of Reggie's property. "If someone needed to hide out for a few days, that would be a good place. There are tunnels and caverns most people don't even know about. No one from around here will go down there anymore. A couple of teenagers lost their way and drowned in an underwater passage years back. Mr. McNally fenced off the entrance and posted a bunch of signs, but it wouldn't be hard to climb over the fence and throw a body down in the pit."

"You've been down there?" Jake asked.

"Back in my younger days when you didn't have to sign a waiver. Some of the passageways are belly crawls and my knees aren't what they used to be. But I could still cover some ground if I take old Blue down there with me." The dog's ears twitched at the sound of his name.

"We'd prefer you not go out on your own, especially into dangerous terrain," Jake said. "We like to keep track of all the volunteers so that no one gets lost and we don't end up covering the same ground twice."

Plus, the criminal background checks required of each volunteer could potentially lead to the kidnapper's identity if he or she decided to join in the search.

Lyle nodded. "Makes sense, I guess."

"You can sign up at the command center we've established at the police station. In the meantime, would you mind answering a few questions while I'm here?"

He seemed agreeable. "I've got no place I need to be anytime soon. But you should know I've already talked to the police. A couple of officers stopped by my place after I got home yesterday. I told them everything I know, which isn't much."

"That's okay. Sometimes something can come back to you a day or two later."

Lyle leaned against the side of the SUV and folded his arms. "Fire away then."

"Were you home Sunday night through early Monday morning?"

He shook his head regretfully. "I wish I had been home. I might have seen something. But I was in Pensacola on a fishing trip with my brother."

"When did you leave on this trip?"

"Saturday morning right around sunrise. I wanted to beat the beach crowd. Drove over to Crestview, picked up my brother, and then we cruised on down to the Gulf. We were on the water all weekend. Didn't hear about the kidnapping until I got home around four or five in the afternoon. That's when the cops came by."

"You didn't get an Amber Alert on your phone Monday morning?"

Lyle rubbed the back of his neck. "Don't think so. I'm sure I would have noticed since the missing kid was local. But we were out on the water early. I probably had my phone turned off. I like peace and quiet when I fish."

"So you were away from your house from early Saturday morning until late yesterday afternoon?"

"That's right. My brother has Mondays off. We had to get back so he could go to work today. He's not retired like I am."

"You didn't see anything out of the ordinary before you left on Saturday? No strangers in the neighborhood or any unfamiliar cars on the street? Maybe someone paying a little too much attention to Reggie's house?"

"I think I would have noticed if someone had been watching Reggie's house."

"They would have been discreet," Jake said. "Maybe you saw the same car drive by her house a few times. Or maybe you noticed workers or repair vans nearby."

"Like I said, I would have noticed anything out of the

ordinary." He opened the lid of the tumbler and tossed out the ice. "I keep a sharp eye out when I'm home."

Jake glanced across the street. "You have a good view of Reggie's property from your front windows. Did you ever see Kylie Buchanan playing in the yard alone?"

A brow lifted. "Alone, no. Why?"

"It could have provided someone the opportunity to approach her, maybe under the pretext of being a neighbor out looking for a lost pet. It's a known ploy," Jake said, his gaze narrowing slightly. "A way to gain her trust."

Lyle shrugged. "Anytime I saw the girl outside, her mother was always hovering nearby. She seemed to watch that kid like a hawk. I didn't know who either of them was until all this happened. I didn't even know Reggie had someone living over there. She has a grown daughter. I thought maybe Thea had had a kid since the last time I'd seen her, and they were down here visiting."

"You didn't recognize Taryn Buchanan? She and her husband, Russ, have lived in Black Creek for the past five years. They have a house in Crescent Hill."

"That area of town is a little rich for my blood. I don't get over that way much." He paused as if something had occurred to him. "How does someone with a house in Crescent Hill end up in this neighborhood living with Reggie Lamb?"

"We're still trying to sort out the details," Jake said. "Do you live alone, Mr. Crowder?"

"If you don't count my coonhound. He's about the only family I have left besides my brother. We get along fine on our own, don't we, Blue?"

The dog's tail flapped lazily.

"How long have you lived across the street?" Jake asked.

"I've owned the property for over thirty years, but I wasn't around for a lot of that time. I worked as an offshore welder before I retired. Spent more time on a platform than I did at home. 'Floating cities,' we called them. I'd sometimes be away for two or three months at a time."

"Were you home when Maya Lamb went missing?"

Lyle Crowder's easygoing demeanor vanished. A wall seemed to go up as he straightened, pretending to move into deeper shade.

"That was a long time ago."

Jake nodded. "Twenty-eight years, to be exact, but you don't forget something like that, especially when it occurs across the street from your home."

An odd note crept into the man's voice; a curious combination of defiance and uncertainty. "Why are you asking about Maya Lamb? You don't think the same person took the Buchanan girl, do you? After all this time?"

"We don't leave any stone unturned when a child goes missing," Jake said.

Lyle's brow furrowed. "Yeah, okay. I remember now. I'd started a new job that summer working on a rig out of New Orleans. I didn't get home much that whole year."

Two little girls had gone missing from the house across the street and Lyle Crowder had conveniently been away each time. For someone who liked to keep an eye out, he seemed to have a knack for making himself scarce when crimes were committed.

"We all heard about the disappearance," he said. "You couldn't turn on the TV or open a paper all summer long without seeing that little girl's picture. There was a lot of speculation about what had happened to her. Like she might have been dead before she went missing, if you know what I mean. But after a while, people lost interest and moved on."

"How well did you know Reggie back then?"

A frown flitted as he studied the front of her house, his expression so intense he might have been peering into one of her windows. Or into her past. "When you live in a small town, you know everybody to a certain degree. Reggie was a lot younger than me, so we didn't socialize much. I guess you could say we were friendly acquaintances. But anyone in Black Creek will tell you she was pretty wild back then."

"What do you mean by 'wild'?"

"Booze and men, men and booze. She kind of went off the deep end after her baby daddy wrapped his car around a light pole one night. Not that he was ever going to marry her anyway. His mother didn't approve. Wrong side of the tracks and all that. After he was killed, June Chapman hardly had anything to do with those little girls. Never offered financial support or anything, and her old man left her loaded. That's pretty cold if you ask me, shunning her own grandkids."

He was getting a little too gossipy, but Jake didn't try to rein him in. He liked to think that his silence would encourage Crowder to let down his guard. But, if he were honest with himself, he'd have to admit he found these peeks into Thea's past riveting. She'd been gone from his life for four years and yet she remained the most enigmatic woman he'd ever known. In all their time together, he'd never been able to figure her out and maybe that was why, in all their time apart, he'd never been able to forget her.

"Reggie must have been young when she had her twins," he said.

"Not much more than a kid herself," Lyle agreed. "You'd think two babies would have slowed her down, but not Reggie. Every Saturday night, she'd have a bunch of people over here to party. Maybe it was her way of thumbing her nose at June Chapman and all the other old biddies in town that looked down on her. She and her friends would crank up the music and hang out in the yard. Somebody would tap a keg or light up a joint. It got pretty rowdy at times. I don't know how those little girls managed to sleep through all the ruckus."

"Did you ever attend any of these parties?"

"Nah. Even if I'd been around, that crowd would have considered me a geezer."

Was that a note of resentment in his voice? A lingering umbrage?

Lyle Crowder's gaze met Jake's then shifted away. "Reggie wasn't much of a mother in a lot of respects, but I'll say this for her. She was always a hard worker. Made sure her kids had clean clothes and plenty to eat. When her landlord died, she managed to scrape together a down payment and somehow convinced his boy to sell her this place. No telling how many double shifts she had to work just to make the mortgage payments. Regardless of her failings, you have to admire her for that."

Jake's eyes roamed the yard. For a moment, he had a vision of two little girls playing on the old tire swing hanging from one of the oak trees. If he listened hard enough, he could almost hear the echo of their forgotten laughter. Then one of the girls vanished and the other erected impenetrable defenses. "Did you see anyone besides Reggie here this morning?"

"If you're asking whether or not I saw who painted that on her wall? No, but it's not the first time some creep tagged her house. You know how it is in a place like this. People have small minds and long memories. Some folks around here still think Reggie was responsible for her daughter's disappearance."

"What do you think?"

He stared broodingly at the faded letters at the side of the porch. "You don't want to believe someone you've known your whole life, let alone someone who lives across the street, could do such a terrible thing to her own child. I mean, Reggie had her faults, and plenty of them, but from what I saw, she loved her kids. If something happened to that little girl before she went missing, it must have been an accident. Reggie was young and impulsive. Maybe she panicked and got rid of the body instead of calling the police."

"Is that what you think happened?"

Lyle shrugged. "It's plausible, isn't it? Although, to tell you the truth, Reggie never struck me as the panicky type. Personally, I've always wondered about that old boy she used to go with."

"Do you remember his name?"

Lyle's mouth curled in contempt. "Derrick Sway. Had such a bad temper, he'd fly off the handle for no apparent reason. Some of that dope will make you real unstable."

"What makes you think he had something to do with Maya's disappearance?" Jake asked.

"Just a gut feeling I've always had. If Sway was somehow responsible for what happened to Maya, I wouldn't put it past him to threaten her sister just to keep Reggie quiet."

"Sounds like you knew Derrick Sway pretty well."

"Everyone in town knew him by reputation. He'd steal anything he could get his hands on. Peddled meth, too, when it was just getting started around here. I never understood how someone with Reggie's looks and smarts could take up with a lowlife like him."

"Do you know if he was at the party the night Maya went missing?"

"That's what I heard, but I can't swear to it since I wasn't here. The cops must have talked to him after it happened. It's probably all in a file somewhere."

"How long did he and Reggie stay together after Maya went missing?"

"Not long. She wised up and kicked his sorry hide to the curb. Maybe she suspected something, I don't know. Rumor had it, he tried to come back a time or two and she chased him off with a shotgun."

"Sounds like there was bad blood between them," Jake said.

Lyle gave a vague nod but his gaze remained wary and shrewd. "Sway spent the next few years in and out of county lockup for one petty crime after another. But the last time he got busted was for armed robbery. That got him a dime over in Lake City. You know about that place, right?"

"The Columbia Correctional Institute is considered one of the most violent prisons in the state of Florida," Jake said.

"You think? You heard about what happened a while back. One of the prisoners strangled his cellmate, mutilated the body and then wore the guy's ears around his neck to breakfast. I'd call that violent, all right. You don't survive a decade on the inside of a place like that without resorting to your baser instincts. Put it this way—now that Derrick Sway's a free man, I wouldn't want to meet up with him in a dark alley. Or on the street in broad daylight, for that matter."

"When did he get out?" Jake asked.

"I don't know. Been a while, I guess. Last I heard, he was living over in Yulee with his mother. Probably freeloading off her social security."

Jake studied Lyle's expression. He seemed genuinely distressed by Derrick Sway's release. "You haven't seen him around Black Creek?"

"Black Creek, no. But about a month or so back, a buddy of mine was fishing on Lake Seminole. He said a man came out of the woods looking all wide-eyed and crazy. Had these crude tattoos on his neck and arms.

Dark stuff like skulls and horns and snakes. Prison gang tats, mostly likely. My friend, Carl, swore the man looked just like Derrick Sway."

"What happened?"

"Nothing. The guy never said a word, just came to the edge of the water and stood there staring at Carl. He thought for a moment that the dude was going to wade out after him. Maybe knock him in the head and steal his boat. Then he just turned and walked back into the woods. Gave Carl the creeps. He hightailed it out of there and never went back to that spot. I didn't give it much thought until you started asking all these questions about Maya's disappearance."

"Do you know the exact location of this sighting?" Jake asked.

"No, but Carl owns a store just south of town. C & C's Tire Service. You can go by there and ask him yourself. Tell him I sent you."

"Thank you, Mr. Crowder. You've been a big help."

"You bet." He thrust a hand in his pocket and jangled some change. "There is one other thing. I don't know if I should even bring it up. Maybe it means something, maybe it doesn't."

"I'm listening."

The jangling stopped and his expression turned grim. "After Sway got arrested, there was talk around town that Reggie was the one who turned him in. If he's carried a grudge against her all these years, God help her. If he had anything to do with that little Buchanan girl's disappearance, God have mercy."

Chapter Two

Lyle Crowder called to his dog and the pair sauntered back across the street, leaving Jake alone in the heat to ponder their conversation. As he waited for the man to disappear into his house, a strange feeling of being watched came over him. That wasn't unusual for Jake. He'd always had a heightened sensitivity to his surroundings that went beyond his training. He'd never put a name to his perception and had no interest in digging deep enough to figure it out. Suffice it to say, he'd learned early on in foster care to trust his instincts. That keen situational awareness had saved him more times than he cared to remember.

Slowly, he trailed his gaze along the row of aging houses as the hair at the back of his neck lifted. Could be nothing more than another nosy neighbor staring out a window. People were curious when something like this happened. They watched from the safety of their homes, telling themselves that something so terrible could never happen to their family. But sometimes the kidnapper also watched.

For all Jake knew, Kylie Buchanan's abductor could

still be in the neighborhood, monitoring police activity from behind closed blinds, reveling in the chaos he'd created and smug in the certainty that he'd outsmarted the authorities.

Rubbing the back of his neck, Jake searched for the twitch of a curtain or the subtle shift of a shadow. Then his eyes moved to Crowder's house. Despite the man's chattiness, Jake sensed Reggie's neighbor hadn't been entirely forthcoming. Reading between the lines, he wondered if Lyle Crowder had had romantic feelings for Reggie in the past. His opinion of her had seemed to vacillate between condemnation and respect, and Jake had detected a flicker of something unpleasant when he spoke about being left out of her parties. Unrequited feelings could sometimes fester into resentment, but thirty years was a long time to carry a grudge or a torch. One thing Jake knew for certain: Lyle Crowder had done everything in his power to focus the FBI's attention on Derrick Sway.

Moving out of view of the street, Jake pulled his phone and called the local police chief to verify that Crowder's brother had corroborated their weekend fishing trip. He then related Lyle's concern about Derrick Sway and requested that an officer be sent to the mother's home to check on Sway's whereabouts. Statistically speaking, Sway was a long shot. Stranger abductions were more rare than most people realized, and Sway had no apparent connection to the Buchanans. He did, however, have a past with Reggie Lamb and, at this point, no lead could be ignored. No one could be ruled out, and that included Reggie herself.

Jake had spoken with her twice since his arrival in town. The first time here at her home. The second time at the command center when she'd come in with Taryn Buchanan. His initial impression was of a hard-boiled woman who spoke her mind regardless of the consequences. Jake had liked her at once and had to remind himself that she was the common denominator in two child abductions. He couldn't afford to cut her any slack because she happened to be Thea's mother.

Still, he'd been at this for a long time and he knew how to read people. He didn't think Reggie was responsible for Kylie Buchanan's disappearance, but he couldn't shake the notion that she was hiding something, too.

So here he was.

Instinct was one thing, but Jake didn't believe in premonitions, second sights or any of that nonsense. He'd never put faith in psychics. Yet something inexplicable had drawn him back to Reggie Lamb's house.

Slipping on his sunglasses, he moved from the shade and dragged his gaze along the edge of the woods. He imagined the kidnapper creeping silently through the trees on the night of the abduction, then hunkering in the shadows until the lights in Reggie's house had gone out. Cloud coverage would have obscured the moon. Even if someone had been passing by at that hour, whoever took four-year-old Kylie Buchanan would have gone undetected as he eased across the yard and peered through the glass before sliding up the window.

The peal of Jake's ringtone shattered the heavy silence. He took the call and ended it quickly. Guided by the prickles at the base of his neck, he let himself in through the gate in the chain-link fence then moved across the backyard to where the woods edged up against Reggie's property line.

A latticework potting shed had been erected behind a detached single-car garage. Both structures looked freshly painted in the same color as the trim on the house. Jake could hear birds trilling in the oak trees and the steady *click-click-click* of an ornamental windmill rotating in the breeze. The yard was like a peaceful oasis, fragrant and sleepy, and yet he felt the heaviness of a strange oppression as he unlatched the back gate and stepped through.

He followed a footpath into the trees. He didn't know what he expected to find. The local police had used K-9 tracking to search the area early Monday morning, and a small army of law enforcement personnel and civilian volunteers walking at arm's length of one another had combed the woods later that same day. Every square inch had been covered. Nothing of importance would have been missed. Jake told himself his time would be better spent at the command center assisting the local PD, yet he couldn't bring himself to turn back. He couldn't assuage the compulsion that drove him deeper into the woods.

A few hundred yards from the house, he halted abruptly, searching the shadowy underbrush and then swinging his scrutiny up into the treetops. A sound had come to him.

Maybe it was that subtle intrusion that had been guiding him through the woods all along rather than any premonition. Maybe, in the back of his mind, he'd conflated the hollow clatter he heard now with the distant tick of the windmill so that his subconscious had dismissed the sound.

He tipped his head, searching for the source. Almost hidden by leaves, two primitive stick figures swung from a tree branch about five feet above his head. Twig arms and legs had been attached to the bodies with coils of raffia. Red fabric hearts had been glued to the torsos and tufts of blond hair to the heads.

Jake watched, mesmerized as the dolls clacked together in the breeze, creating an eerie, hollow melody that reminded him of a bamboo wind chime.

THEA RECLINED HER head against the back of the seat and tried to relax as Reggie exited the freeway onto the state highway that would take them straight into Black Creek. But the closer they drew to their destination, the more anxious she became.

She kept the window open, pulling the damp, verdant smell of the countryside deep into her lungs. The scent stirred something powerful inside her. The memories that stole out of her subconscious were as thick and pervasive as the kudzu that snaked up abandoned utility poles and curled around old phone lines. There was something almost mystical about that lush perfume, something evocative and sinister about the shadowy landscape.

She gave her mother a sidelong glance. Did she feel it, too?

Seemingly oblivious, Reggie gripped the wheel and stared straight ahead. They'd both fallen silent miles ago. Thea didn't try to initiate further conversation.

She welcomed a few minutes of quiet introspection to analyze her feelings. It was so disconcerting, this homecoming. She hadn't been in the same room with her mother in years, let alone in the close confines of a vehicle. Now here they were with all the old doubts and resentments crowding into the same narrow space.

How long had it been since she'd been back anyway? Four years? Five? Surely not six? Where had all that time gone?

The odd thing was, she and Reggie had never had a real falling out. The distancing had been gradual. Phone calls had tapered off, visits had never come to fruition. It was just plain easier being apart. Easier to ignore the ghost that had always haunted the space between them.

Maya's abduction had defined their relationship in so many ways, yet even the mention of her name had at times been taboo. Thea had learned early on to keep any questions about her sister's disappearance to herself if she didn't want Reggie to shut down. Those long silences had taken a toll.

You freeze a kid out enough times and she'll put up her own defenses. She'll find all kinds of ways to act out and then she'll leave home as soon as she's able, rarely to return until another child goes missing.

Thea didn't want to dwell on all those old doubts. She didn't want to resurrect her obsession over her twin sister's abduction, but how could she not when another child had gone missing from the same room? When little Kylie Buchanan might still be out there somewhere, tormented and terrified and crying for her mother as Maya had undoubtedly done before she died?

She took a long, tremulous breath and allowed her mind to drift back in time.

On the night of Maya's disappearance, Reggie had put them to bed early. Twilight had just fallen, but already music and laughter drifted in from the front porch where some of her friends had gathered. Thea didn't like it when her mother had people over. She and Maya were always sent to bed early and Thea had a hard time sleeping through all that noise. Bored and fretful, she'd lie awake for hours while Maya slept peacefully in the next bed.

Their room had been exceptionally hot and sticky that night. The AC unit in the front part of the house did nothing to cool the bedrooms. Thea lay on top of the covers, hot and miserable as she tossed and turned. Sometime later, Reggie came into the room to raise the window that looked out on the backyard.

"Read me a story, Mama."

"Not tonight, baby. Your sister's already asleep and I don't want to wake her up. Besides, Mama has friends over."

"I don't like them." Thea pouted. "They smell bad."

"That's just cigarette smoke. The breeze will blow it away. Now settle down and go to sleep. It'll be morning before you know it."

Thea pretended to do as she was told. She nestled under the covers and watched her mother through half-closed eyes as she stood at the open window staring out into the night. After a moment, Reggie came over to the bed and kissed Thea's cheek, then tiptoed from the room and pulled the door closed behind her.

At the sound of the clicking door, her sister sat up in bed and whimpered. "I'm scared, Sissy."

"Why?" Thea asked her.

"I heard something."

Thea listened to the night. "It's just a coonhound out in the woods. See? Mama opened the window."

"It's not a coonhound." Kicking off the covers, Maya slid to the floor and padded the short distance between their beds. Clutching her favorite doll, she crawled beneath the cotton sheets and snuggled close. "Somebody's out there, Sissy."

"Nobody's out there. Stop being a fraidy-cat and go back to sleep." Thea patted her sister's shoulder until Maya finally rolled over and drifted off. Thea remained wide awake. Despite the breeze, she was still too hot with her sister's clammy little body pressed up against hers. The open window allowed in dozens of night sounds. Not just the eerie baying of a neighbor's dog, but also the closer serenades of crickets and bullfrogs and the occasional hoot of an owl. Sounds that stirred Thea's blood and tingled her scalp.

She slipped out of bed and dragged a chair to the window so that she could stand and stare out the way her mother had done. For the longest time, she watched shadows dance across the yard as tree limbs thrashed in the breeze. When she grew drowsy, she climbed into Maya's empty bed and pulled the covers to her chin, and when she finally fell asleep, she dreamed the outside shadows had crept into their room and stood whispering between their beds.

The next thing she knew, it was morning and her

mother's best friend, Gail, was shaking her awake. "Where's your sister? Thea, wake up! Where's Maya?"

They searched the house and all up and down the street. The police came and later the FBI. Search parties were formed and dogs were brought in.

A week after Maya went missing, a wooden box had been found in the woods containing her doll and a bloodstained blanket that matched her DNA. The police reasoned but couldn't prove that Maya had been buried in the box and her body later dug up and moved to a more remote location.

They'd dragged Reggie back in for questioning, along with her boyfriend, Derrick Sway. Eventually, they'd both been released, but suspicions lingered in Black Creek. Those dark whispers had dogged Thea all through school, at times poking at the doubts that dwelled at the fringes of her memory.

She'd managed to put her misgivings aside when she left her hometown for college. Those four years had been the most peaceful time of her young life. But then, as a federal agent, she'd been able to access Maya's file. In Reggie's official statement, she'd neglected to mention her second trip into the bedroom to raise the window. Maybe the oversight had been an honest mistake. In the shock and horror of her daughter's disappearance, she could have easily forgotten the sequence of events. It was a small thing, really. Hardly worth thinking about in the scheme of things.

Yet Thea knew only too well that what went unspoken was often far more important than the information revealed in any interview or statement.

And that seemingly insignificant omission had started to niggle at her again.

"Why are you staring at me?" Reggie demanded.

Her voice jolted Thea from her deep reverie and she physically started. "What? I'm sorry. I was lost in thought. I didn't realize I was staring."

Reggie gave her a quizzical look. "What were you thinking about so hard?"

Thea answered without hesitation. "The abduction. You were going to tell me how Taryn and Kylie Buchanan came to be living with you."

Her mother turned her eyes back to the road. "Like I said, it's a long story. I hardly know where to start."

"How did you meet?" Thea prompted.

"They started attending my church a few weeks ago. We have a new preacher and a lot of folks have been coming to check him out. The kids adore him. I think even you would approve of Brother Eldon. He's already done a lot for the community and he's been a godsend to Taryn."

That got Thea's attention. "How so?"

"He's counseled her all through the separation with her husband. Been there for her every step of the way. I don't know if she could have handled the stress without him. He got her a job at the church so that she could keep Kylie with her all day, and he even helped her find a little apartment in town. She and Taryn were supposed to move in at the end of the week. Since the police are treating my house as a crime scene, the landlord let her stay there last night. Brother Eldon has barely left her side since Kylie went missing."

"Are they romantically involved?" Thea asked bluntly.

The question seemed to rub Reggie the wrong way. "Now why would you ask a thing like that? Don't turn a good deed into something dirty."

Thea put up a hand. "Sorry. No need to get defensive. I'm not accusing or judging, just trying to get the full picture. But we're getting ahead of ourselves anyway. Let's go back. You met Taryn and Kylie at church…"

Reggie nodded. "They started coming on Wednesday nights, which I thought a little odd. We typically have a short service on that night followed by church business. We hardly ever have visitors. Nonmembers almost always come for Sunday morning service."

"Why did she come on Wednesday nights?"

"She told me later her husband frequently stayed overnight in Tallahassee on Wednesday nights. Anyway, Taryn would sit at the very back, clutching little Kylie's hand and glancing over her shoulder as if she were afraid someone would burst through the door and snatch the child away from her." Reggie paused as reality sank in. "I could tell she needed a friend, so I made a point of speaking to her after every service."

"What happened then?"

"She and Kylie came into the diner one day. She asked if we could talk. I took my break and we walked across the street to the park where we could speak in private. She was shy at first, and maybe a little embarrassed about her situation. Then everything just came pouring out of her. She told me that she'd only been nineteen when she and Russ Buchanan first got together. Her mother had died when she was a kid and her father had passed at the end of her senior year. She used the little dab of money left after his burial to move to Tallahassee where she could find steady work. Russ was older, handsome and charming, and already a successful lawyer. He saw her in the lobby of his office building one day and swept her off her feet. They were married two months later."

"Let me guess," Thea said. "Things didn't work out as she'd hoped."

"Same old story," Reggie said with a heavy sigh. "Butter wouldn't melt in his mouth until he had her under his spell. She was exactly the type of vulnerable young woman men like him prey on. He moved her into a house he bought in Black Creek, away from everyone she knew in Tallahassee. He started asking her to dress a certain way, wear her hair a certain way, cook his meals and clean his house a certain way. Then he stopped asking.

"By the time Taryn realized the kind of man she'd married, she was pregnant and had nowhere else to go. Everything was in Russ's name, of course. The house, the cars, the bank accounts. He gave her an allowance, but she had to justify every penny she spent. When he stayed overnight in Tallahassee, he'd check the mileage on her car when he got home. Things only got worse after the baby came. He threatened to take Kylie away from her if she ever tried to leave him."

"Was he physically abusive?"

"I'm sure he was, though she claims he only grabbed her arm and pushed her around a bit."

"Only?" Thea looked at her mother. "You think she downplayed the level of violence?"

Reggie's expression tightened. "That's my suspicion. She was clearly terrified of him. I told her things would only get worse if she stayed. She needed to go home, pack her bags and get Kylie out of that situation before something truly bad happened. I offered them a place to stay for as long as they needed it."

"You weren't afraid a man like that would try to retaliate against you?" Thea asked.

Her mother lifted a hand from the steering wheel. "What was he going to do to me that hadn't already been done?"

Thea felt a little tremor go through her. "Go on."

"A few nights later, Taryn and Kylie showed up on my doorstep with their suitcases," Reggie said. "I put Kylie in your old room and Taryn slept on the couch. I don't know how Russ found out where they were so quickly. Maybe he had someone watching her or maybe he planted some kind of tracker on her car. When I saw him pull up the next morning, I called the cops and then met him on the front porch. He pushed me aside and kicked open the door. He grabbed Taryn and tried to drag her outside with poor little Kylie screaming bloody murder in the corner. It was a horrible scene. Thank God a patrol car was nearby. I don't know what would have happened if the cops hadn't come when they had."

"Did they take him into custody?"

"No. You know how that goes. A guy like Russ Buchanan has pull even in a place like Black Creek. One of his golfing buddies is a state senator. The cops finally managed to calm him down and got him to leave. Chief Bowden advised Taryn to take out a restraining order, but she was afraid that would only trigger his anger. Things quieted down for a bit. Russ didn't give her any more trouble. He even called ahead the one time he wanted to see Kylie. Taryn was hopeful for a peaceful divorce. And then Kylie went missing. Now Russ blames her for everything."

"Of course he does. Tell me everything you can remember about the day Kylie disappeared."

Reggie nodded. "I had to work. Normally, I have Sundays off, but one of the other girls called in sick and I agreed to take her shift. By the time I got home that evening, I was bone-tired. Taryn was getting ready to go to the evening service and I told her Kylie could stay home with me. Both of them had been through so much, I thought Taryn might enjoy some time to herself. But she said Brother Eldon had a surprise for Kylie that night."

"What kind of surprise?"

"He and some of the other members of the congregation had erected new playground equipment behind the church and he promised Kylie she could be the first one down the slide. After they left, I took a bath and went straight to bed. I was so tired, I didn't even hear them come home. The next thing I knew, Taryn was standing over my bed screaming that Kylie was gone. I got up and ran into the bedroom. When I saw the open window—" She stopped short and drew a sharp breath. "I knew what had happened. I knew it was just like before."

Thea's pulse thudded as her mind went back to that night. "Was the window open when Taryn put Kylie to bed?"

"That window is kept closed and locked at all times."

"Are you certain Taryn didn't go in sometime later and open it to let in some fresh air?" Thea turned to stare at her mother as she waited for her response.

"There's no reason why she would have. I had central AC installed in the house years ago. The bedrooms stay plenty cool."

"Had the lock been jimmied?" Thea asked.

"The police said there was no sign of a forced entry anywhere in the house."

"Who has a key besides you?"

"No one. Taryn has been using the spare I keep in a flowerpot on my front porch."

"Would she put it back after each use?"

Reggie glanced at her. "The police checked. It was still there on Monday morning. Why?"

"If someone was watching your house, they would have seen her take the key out of the flowerpot and return it. They could have waited until you were both out of the house, let themselves in and unlocked the bedroom window."

Reggie returned her attention to the road. "Someone like Russ Buchanan, you mean."

"Considering his previous threats and behavior, I'm sure the police are giving him a hard look."

Her mother scoffed at the suggestion. "For all the good it will do. I told you he has pull. If he took Kylie, they'll never be able to pin it on him."

"What makes you so sure?"

A bitter edge crept into Reggie's voice. "Because bad men do bad things and get away with it all the time."

"Not all the time," Thea said. "The prisons are full of bad men who did bad things and got caught."

"Not men like Russ Buchanan."

They both fell silent after that. Thea shifted her attention to the outside mirror where she could watch the road behind them. A black pickup had been following them ever since they'd exited the freeway. She hadn't given much thought to it earlier, but now she realized that the vehicle had been maintaining the same distance between them.

"Check out the vehicle behind us," she said.

Reggie glanced in the rearview mirror. "The black pickup? What about it?"

"I'm wondering if it's the same vehicle that cut you off at the airport."

Reggie took another perusal. "I doubt it. Trucks are a dime a dozen in this part of the state. Be a pretty big coincidence if that truck was headed in our direction."

Thea kept her gaze on the mirror. "Normally, I would agree, but the driver has been keeping pace with us for several miles. Just seems odd to me."

"Why? We're both doing the speed limit."

"Give it a little gas," Thea said. "I want to see if he falls behind."

"Are you going to pay my speeding ticket?" Reggie demanded.

"I said a little gas. No need to floor it."

Reggie mumbled something under her breath as she pressed down on the pedal.

After a moment, the truck faded.

"See there? Nothing to worry about. Your job is making you paranoid."

"I prefer to think of it as cautious." Thea turned to glance over her shoulder. "Do you happen to know if Russ Buchanan owns a black truck?"

"He's not the pickup truck type. He drove a silver Mercedes when he came to the house." She flashed Thea an uneasy glance. "What are you getting at? You think Russ is having us tailed? Why would he do that?"

"Could be an intimidation thing. You took in his wife and child. It's possible he blames you for Taryn leaving him." Or maybe Russ Buchanan had heard the rumors about Reggie and suspected her of harming his daughter.

No sooner had the thought occurred to Thea than the vehicle appeared once more in the outside mirror. It was coming up fast behind them.

"Reggie—"

"I see him. What do you want me to do?"

"Nothing. Maintain your current speed. If he tries to pass, let him."

Reggie frowned. "What if he tries to ram us?"

"That would be pretty brazen in broad daylight."

"Brazen or not, he's coming up behind us hell-bent for leather." Reggie gripped the wheel as she flicked another glance in the rearview mirror.

Thea turned to track the pickup through the back window. The vehicle was close enough now she could see that the grille and front bumper were splattered with mud, partially concealing the license plate number. She hadn't noticed any mud on the truck at the airport, but then, she'd been distracted by the awkward reunion with her mother. Still, an obscured license plate would have surely caught her attention.

"I keep a .38 in the glove box," Reggie said.

Thea turned at that. "I hope you're not suggesting I open fire."

Her mother met her gaze. "I'm just saying, it's there if we need it."

Thea leaned back against the seat and checked the vehicle in the outside mirror. The driver continued to gain ground. Reggie reflexively sped up.

"Don't try to outrun him," Thea warned. "Let him go around."

The driver edged up as close to Reggie's bumper as he dared without making contact. Then he whipped the truck into the left lane and drew up beside her. For a moment, they were dead even on the two-lane highway. Thea tried to get a look at the driver, but he wore a cap and sunglasses and kept his head turned so that she could make out little more than his silhouette.

"Ease up on the gas," she told Reggie.

Before the pickup could pass, another vehicle came barreling around a curve in front of them. Reggie hit the brakes to allow the truck room to merge into the right lane, but the driver swerved too early, sideswiping Reggie's car and sending them careening onto the shoulder. The rear end fishtailed as the tires whirled in loose gravel.

Reggie fought to maneuver the car back onto pavement, but the momentum of the spin plunged them down the embankment toward a line of trees. Everything seemed to happen in the blink of an eye. Thea caught a glimpse of her mother's tense face a split second be-

fore they hit a rock and the car went airborne. She tried
to brace herself, leaning deep into the seat and folding
her arms over her chest. She would later remember a
strange feeling of weightlessness. Then the car bounced
off the ground and rolled.

When the world finally stopped spinning, she was
still buckled into her seat in the upside-down vehicle.

Dazed, she sat quietly for a moment, trying to recali-
brate her nervous system as the airbags deflated. Then
she ran her hands over her head to check for blood and
broken glass. *You're okay. You're okay.*

She glanced at Reggie and her heart almost stopped.
Her mother was slumped sideways, motionless. Thea
touched her shoulder. "Reggie? You okay?"

No answer.

Don't panic.

As if in slow motion, Thea reached over and shut off
the engine while simultaneously searching for the cross-
body bag containing her phone. Bracing one hand on
the ceiling and her feet against the floor, she snapped
off her seat belt and crawled through the open window.
By the time she managed to stagger to her feet, a man
was running down the embankment toward her. She
checked the side of the road and saw a dark blue SUV.
The black pickup was nowhere in sight.

"Hey!" he called out. "Everybody okay?"

Thea fumbled in her bag for her phone. "My mother's
unconscious inside the vehicle."

"I called 9-1-1 as soon as I saw the collision. An ambulance is on the way," he said.

Thea hurried around the car and dropped to the ground

beside the window, keeping the newcomer in her line of sight while trying to take stock of Reggie's injuries. She had a deep cut on her upper arm that bled profusely. Thea reached for her mother's wrist to check for a pulse.

"I work for the fire department," the man told her as he hunkered down beside her and glanced through the window. "We shouldn't try to move her until the EMTs get here. Spinal chord injuries are always a danger in this type of accident."

"Her pulse is thready," Thea said. "Her skin feels clammy."

"She may be in shock from blood loss." The man whipped off his shirt and pressed the folded fabric to Reggie's arm. "Can you keep up the pressure? I've got a first aid kit and a blanket in my truck."

Thea nodded and took over. She glanced up as the man stood. "What happened to the vehicle that hit us?"

"Kept going and never looked back." He gazed down at her. "You sure you're okay?"

"Yes, but please hurry."

After he left, Thea adjusted her position so she had better access through the window. She talked to her mother as she applied pressure to the wound. "You're going to be fine. Help is on the way."

Blood soaked through the stranger's shirt onto Thea's hands. "The ambulance will be here any minute now. Just stay with me, okay?"

She tried to bite back her panic, but Reggie was so pale, and her lips were turning blue. *Oh, please don't die. Please, please, please don't die.* "You hear me, Mama? Don't you die on me."

Chapter Three

After an anxious dash through the maze of hospital corridors, Jake finally found Thea in the surgical waiting room. She stood staring out a window with her back to the entrance. He called her name softly as he approached. He didn't want to catch her off guard, but she jumped and whirled as if startled by unexpected gunfire.

Her blue eyes went wide when she saw him, and something flashed a split second before she glanced away. Jake didn't want to put a name to the emotion for fear he'd imagined the tiny flare. But he could have sworn her initial response to his presence had been relief. Perhaps even happiness. He was going with that.

She controlled her visible reaction as she gave him a puzzled frown. "Jake! What are you doing here?"

"Chief Bowden told me what happened. I wanted to see for myself that you're okay." His heart dropped in spite of himself as he took in the cuts and bruises on her face and the bloodstained white blouse. *Talk about trying to hide your visible reaction.* "Damn, Thea."

"It looks worse than it is." She brushed back a loose

strand of dark blond hair from her forehead. "I'm fine. Most of the blood isn't mine."

"How's your mother?"

"She regained consciousness in the ambulance, so that's a good sign. She has cuts and bruises, and the CT scan showed some internal bleeding. They took her into surgery a little while ago."

"I'm surprised they didn't transport her to Tallahassee," Jake said.

"Black Creek General was closer, and she'd already lost a lot of blood. This is a good hospital." Her expression turned apprehensive as she glanced at the clock on the wall. "But it seems to be taking forever. You know how it is when you're waiting. Time crawls."

Jake nodded. "Why don't I go see if I can find out anything?"

"No, that's okay. They'll let me know when there's an update. I would like to go wash my face, though. Do you mind waiting in case someone comes to find me?"

"Take your time."

As Jake watched her disappear down the hallway, he found himself reflecting on how long it had been since he'd last seen her. Four years and some change, but in a way it seemed as if no time had passed at all. She was still a swimmer judging by her lithe figure and sinewy muscle tone. Still practical in her manner of dress and demeanor, yet even in bloodstained clothing, Thea Lamb had an allure that went well beyond the physical. Tough as nails when she needed to be and unflinching in the face of danger, but Jake had seen her break down inconsolably at the sight of an injured kitten. She mostly kept that side of her personality hidden. It was there, though, beneath the battle-hardened surface, and he could only imagine what a decade of working crimes against children had done to her. To him, too, for that matter. Their defenses were strong for a reason.

He gave her a benign smile when she came back into the room, though all he could think about was how much he wanted to wrap his arms around her. Now was not the time or place, of course. Too many years had gone by and Thea had never been demonstrative even when the smallest of gestures would have kept him in DC for as long as she wanted him there.

Water under the bridge. "You've had someone look at your injuries, right? That cut above your eye looks pretty deep."

"What?" She put a hand to her face. "Yes. They removed glass fragments in the ER and gave me a tetanus shot. No stitches required. Reggie's side of the vehicle got the worst of it."

"Can you tell me what happened?"

"I can, but I already gave a statement to one of the officers at the scene. It should be in his report."

"I'd like to hear it from you."

She looked as if she might refuse his request then she shrugged. "A vehicle trying to pass swerved into our car to avoid oncoming traffic. He knocked us onto the shoulder, we spun out in loose gravel and Reggie lost control."

"Can you describe the vehicle and driver? Or better yet, did you get a plate number?"

"I really didn't get a good look at the driver. He wore

a baseball cap and sunglasses, and he kept his head turned toward the road, so I only glimpsed his profile. He was white and I had the impression he was middle-aged or older—in his fifties maybe—and heavyset. Heavyset as in brawny. Muscular. The vehicle was a late-model black pickup truck with chrome wheels. I didn't get the make, and the grille and bumper area was splattered with mud, so the plate was partly hidden."

"Deliberately hidden would you say?"

She hesitated. "Possibly. The rest of the truck looked fairly clean. I remember noticing the shiny paint. I'd been watching the vehicle in the outside mirror for a while before the accident. I thought it strange that the driver kept the same distance between us mile after mile. There were hardly any other cars on the road and Reggie was driving the speed limit. Most people go a few miles over, especially in a vehicle like that. I asked her to speed up to see if he would do the same. He dropped out of sight for a minute and then he came up behind us quickly. That's when he tried to pass."

"How long do you think he'd been following you?" Jake asked.

"At least since we left the freeway."

"Did the driver have any distinguishing marks? Piercings or tattoos? Scars? Anything like that?"

"None that I noticed. As I said, I only had a glance." She gave him a long scrutiny. "Why all these questions, Jake? Do you know something I don't?"

He said uneasily, "Emotions are running high in this town. There was an incident at Reggie's house."

"The vandalism?" Thea nodded. "She told me. Do

you have a suspect? Is that why you're asking about scars and tattoos?"

"We don't have a suspect. Apparently it was painted late last night or early this morning under cover of darkness."

"And you're thinking the two incidents are somehow related?"

"I'm not thinking anything at the moment," Jake said. "I'm just trying to put the information together."

Her blue eyes looked troubled and faintly disapproving. "Okay. But why are you involved at all? The local police have jurisdiction over the vandalism and the Florida Highway Patrol over the accident. Why not let them do their jobs? Your sole focus should be on finding Kylie Buchanan."

Her censure touched a nerve. "She is my sole focus," Jake said quietly. "I assure you, everything that can be done is being done to find that little girl."

Thea looked contrite. "I'm sorry. That didn't come out the way I intended. I'm not questioning your integrity or your priorities. No one is better at this job than you are. I just meant…" She glanced down at her hands and shrugged. "I guess I'm wondering why you're really here. You could have easily called to check up on me."

"I could have," he agreed. "And you're right, I do have an ulterior motive."

"Which is…?"

He hesitated, choosing his words carefully. "Your perspective on this case is unique. Considering your history and Reggie's connection, it shouldn't be surprising that I'd seek you out." *In spite of* our *history.*

"When you put it that way…" She looked tense and her voice sounded strained. "How can I help?"

He motioned to a pair of uncomfortable-looking chairs. "Let's sit."

She gave a weary nod and sat facing the entrance. Her gaze went back to the clock as Jake took the seat beside her.

"You want some coffee?" he asked.

"I'm fine."

"You've been through a lot. Would you rather I come back later?"

"No, but before we start, can you at least catch me up? Reggie filled me in on her end, but I don't know what's going on regarding the overall search. I assume there's no real news or you wouldn't be here asking for my perspective."

"You know the procedure." Jake ran fingers through his hair as he shifted impatiently. "We're still conducting canvasses and we've set up vehicle checkpoints on all the main roads. For the past day and a half, we've had choppers and drones in the air, but the area is heavily wooded with dozens of creeks, lakes and sloughs. It would take weeks to search them all."

"Lots of places for someone to disappear," Thea said worriedly. "Do you think there's a chance she's still alive? The timeline isn't working in her favor."

"She's alive unless and until we recover a body," he said with grim resolve.

Their gazes locked.

"Three percent," Thea murmured.

He nodded. "Three percent."

Neither of them said anything for a long moment but Jake knew the statistics were rolling around in her head just as they were his.

In seventy-four percent of stranger abductions, the victims were found dead within three hours after being reported missing. After twenty-four hours, the number rose to eighty percent and leaped to a staggering ninety-seven percent after a week. Kylie Buchanan had already been missing for thirty-two hours. They were rapidly approaching the point where everyone involved in the search began to cling to the three percent of victims found alive days after they'd been taken.

"Forget about numbers," Thea said. "What does your gut tell you? You always have a feel for how these things will go."

"Not this time."

"Why is that?"

He hesitated, unable to verbalize the disturbing vibes he was getting from some of the people connected to Kylie Buchanan any more than he could explain his visit to Reggie's house earlier that day and the inexplicable pull that had lured him into the woods. "It's an unusual case," was all he said.

Thea looked as if she wanted to press him further, but the surgeon came into the room and Jake heard her catch her breath as she instinctively reached for his hand. The contact shocked him to his core. Earlier he'd wanted nothing so much as to wrap a comforting arm around her shoulders, but now his first instinct was to pull away. His defenses were strong, too. Then he squeezed her fingers in reassurance as they both rose to meet the doctor.

THE SURGEON INTRODUCED himself as he came forward. "I'm Dr. Vaughn. You're Miss Lamb's daughter?"

"Yes, I'm Thea." She realized she was still clinging to Jake's hand. Embarrassed, she let him go and folded her arms over her chest. "How is she?"

"Your mother's a strong woman. She came through surgery like a champ. She's stable and her vitals look good. We'll keep a close eye on the concussion for the next twenty-four to forty-eight hours, but if all goes well, you should be able to take her home by the end of the week."

"When can I see her?"

"She'll be in recovery for a while yet. You can see her as soon as she's moved upstairs."

"Thank you, Dr. Vaughn."

He shook her hand, nodded to Jake and then left the room.

"Good news." Jake gave her a warm smile. "I know you're relieved."

"I am." Thea kept her arms folded at her chest as if she could protect herself from his smile. It had always done things to her, that smile. The way his lips turned up slightly at the corners. The way a single dimple appeared now and then in his right cheek. "I'll feel even better when I can see her," she said.

"It won't be long. In the meantime, are you sure I can't buy you a cup of coffee? The cafeteria is just down the hall from the lobby. You look like you could use a boost."

Thea started to decline, but the adrenaline from the crash had long since worn off and she was starting to deflate. A jolt of caffeine would keep her going for another few hours.

She glanced down at her bloodstained blouse. "I don't know how welcome I'll be in the cafeteria, but I don't have anything with me to change into."

Jake shrugged. "You're in a hospital. If they can't handle a little blood, they're in the wrong line of work."

Thankfully, the cafeteria was nearly empty. Thea found a table in a discrete corner while Jake bought the coffee. He fitted the disposable cups with lids and carried them over.

"You still take it black?"

"Yes." She took a tentative sip and cringed.

"Tastes a little like tar smells," he said as he took the seat across from her. "But it's hot and strong."

"It'll do." Thea cradled the cup in her hands. "What about leads?"

He glanced up from pouring a healthy dose of creamer into his coffee. "What?"

"You were telling me about the investigation before the doctor came in. You must have narrowed down your suspect list by now."

"Not as much as we'd hoped." He stirred his coffee and replaced the lid on his cup. "We're still in the process of tracking down and interviewing anyone who had contact with Kylie or her mother in the days leading up to the abduction. Friends, neighbors, acquaintances. We're still hoping someone may have seen or heard something. We've also identified and located all the known sex offenders in the area, but that angle hasn't been helpful so far." He looked frustrated and worried.

"The truth is, we just don't have much to go on. No fingerprints or trace evidence left at the crime scene. No eyewitness accounts. It's like she vanished into thin air."

"No child ever vanishes into thin air," Thea said.

Another look passed between them. Another flash of understanding.

Thea had forgotten about the unspoken communication she and Jake had once shared, those brief, tender moments of solidarity. They'd spent so much of their time convincing themselves and each other they had no need of a meaningful relationship that they'd failed to appreciate the depth and rarity of their camaraderie. Over the years, Thea had tried not to dwell on how much she missed Jake's friendship, but the loss hit her now as forcefully as the car crash. She took another sip of bad coffee while she tried to regain her composure.

She glanced across the table. Jake stared back at her, his brown eyes so dark and intense her heart thumped. *So much for composure.*

She pretended to adjust the lid on her cup so she could break eye contact. "What about Russ Buchanan? According to Reggie, he physically abused his wife and threatened to take Kylie away from her if she tried to leave him. Reggie said he made a terrible scene when he found out Taryn and Kylie were staying with her."

"We've talked to Buchanan at his home and at the police station. He's arrogant and smug, and seems to think he's untouchable, but he's been cooperative for the most part and his story never changes. Both he and his assistant swear they were together in his Tallahassee apartment on the night of and the morning after Kylie's disappearance. They dined out at a local restaurant on Sunday night and several people saw them arrive at the office together early Monday morning."

"Sounds like they made sure they were seen together. It wouldn't be the first time an employee having an affair with her boss gave him an alibi." Thea watched two nurses come into the cafeteria. They didn't pay the slightest attention to her shirt. They did, however, notice Jake. She could hardly blame them. He was a good-looking man, tall, fit and in the prime of his life at thirty-four. "Even if the assistant is telling the truth, it doesn't necessarily put Buchanan in the clear. A man with his resources wouldn't get his own hands dirty. He has motive and apparently the means to create the opportunity."

"We've got eyes on him," Jake assured her.

"And Taryn?"

She watched in fascination as something inexplicable flashed across Jake's face.

"Now that's interesting." She folded her arms on the table as she searched his expression.

"What is?"

"Your reaction when I asked about Taryn."

He took a moment to answer. "She's hard to read. More difficult in some ways than her husband. Something is going on with her. The fear is palpable, and I'd swear genuine. She's obviously terrified for her child."

"But?"

He gave her a brooding frown. "I can't help wondering about the real source of her fear."

"Meaning?"

He leaned in, lowering his voice as his dark eyes met

Thea's. "She took Kylie to church on Sunday night. More than a dozen people say they saw them together on the playground and later inside the sanctuary. But a witness who left early and drove back after the service to retrieve a forgotten umbrella claims she saw Taryn exit the building, get in her car and drive away without Kylie."

"What does Taryn say?"

"She went back inside to collect some paperwork from the office. Kylie was asleep in the back seat and she didn't want to wake her. She says the child was alone in the car for no more than a couple of minutes."

"You don't believe her?"

"One of Reggie's neighbors said that Taryn was always hovering nearby anytime Kylie played in the front yard. She wouldn't let the child out of her sight." Jake paused as he absently swirled his coffee. "Leaving her daughter alone in the car at night, even for a couple of minutes, doesn't exactly jibe with this neighbor's observation."

"And Reggie was asleep when they got home that night. She said she didn't hear them come in." Now it was Thea who leaned forward. "What are you saying, Jake? Do you think Taryn had something to do with her daughter's disappearance?"

A mask dropped over his expression. "All I can say is that we're exploring every possibility."

"Don't do that," she grumbled.

"Do what?"

"Shut me out. You're the one who wanted my perspective, remember?"

He hesitated then nodded. "Fair enough. I'd like to hear what you think of what I just told you."

Thea shrugged. "I haven't talked to Taryn Buchanan. I've never even met her, so all I can do is speculate. But something occurred to me while you were describing her behavior. It won't make a lot of sense at first, but hear me out."

"I'm listening."

"Do you remember Operation Innocent Images?"

"Yes, of course. It was an undercover operation, launched back in the nineties, that identified and tracked predators through chat rooms and electronic bulletin boards. The expanded program eventually brought down entire networks of online pedophiles and the producers and distributors of child pornography. It became the Innocent Images National Initiative when it was absorbed into the Violent Crimes Against Children unit.

"One of the agents I've been working with in Cold Cases came from Operation Innocent Images. That's how long she's been tracking missing children. She has a theory that an underground railroad for at-risk kids of a tender age has been active in various parts of the country for at least thirty years. The people involved operate exclusively from the shadows. They step in when the system fails."

"How does it work?"

"I'll give you one example. Someone from the organization approaches a woman in a similar situation to Taryn Buchanan's. The contact can be made directly or through an intermediary. The woman has already exhausted every legal means available to protect herself and her child. She's desperate and has no place to turn to for help. The police and courts have either been powerless to help her or are too slow to react.

"The underground operative presents a plan of last resort and if the mother agrees, her child goes missing. Vanishes into thin air," Thea said with a note of irony. "He or she is moved through a series of safe houses until the dust settles and the mother and child can eventually be reunited with new identities. It's much more complicated than I've made it sound, but you get the gist."

"Who are the operatives?" Jake asked.

"Social workers, police officers, FBI and Homeland Security agents. People in trusted positions with wide-ranging resources. Professionals who've seen firsthand what goes on inside the system, and have figured out a way to work around it when a child is in imminent danger. If both parents have failed the child, a friend or family member is sometimes contacted to make the arrangements. The child is then kept hidden until a permanent home can be found and a new identity established."

"Does money change hands?"

"Sometimes. Which means no matter how noble the intent, an operation of this nature is ripe for exploitation."

"And vulnerable to the infiltration of child traffickers, I would think."

"The fastest growing criminal enterprise in the world," she said with a grim nod. "The sheer number of trafficked children worldwide is mind-blowing, Jake."

"You think this group accounts for some of your cold cases?"

"We think it's a very real possibility," Thea said. "Let's suppose for a moment that someone approached Taryn with a way to remove her and Kylie from Russ

Buchanan's reach forever. It could explain why, despite her genuine fear, you've picked up on something from her that doesn't ring true. It could also explain why you have a witness that saw her leave church on Sunday night without Kylie."

He seemed to ponder the possibility. "A plan like that would be risky in any number of ways. The person making the approach would have to be someone Taryn trusted implicitly. Someone with intimate knowledge of her situation. I take it you have someone like that in mind?"

"The preacher at her church is new to the area and has evidently been quite helpful. According to Reggie, he and Taryn have grown very close very quickly. He helped her find an apartment and even arranged a job for her at the church so that she could keep Kylie with her during the day. Also, according to Reggie, he hasn't left Taryn's side since Kylie went missing."

"His name is Eldon Mossey," Jake said. "We've looked into him. He doesn't have a criminal record."

"I wouldn't expect him to. Although he could be using an alias."

"All the database searches came back clean, including CODIS. But the phone number he provided for his former church in Butler, Georgia, has been disconnected."

Thea sat back. "There's a red flag."

"Could be. The Atlanta division is sending an agent from their Macon office to see what he can turn up." Jake studied her for a moment.

She frowned at the scrutiny. "What?"

"We both know of someone else in town that Taryn trusted."

"You mean Reggie." Thea tucked a strand of hair behind her ears. "I figured you'd get around to her sooner or later."

"Given her personal experience with your sister's abduction, it's not hard to imagine how protective she'd feel toward a child she perceived to be in danger."

Thea's defense was automatic. "She doesn't fit the profile. She wouldn't have the know-how or resources to pull off something like that. And, besides, I can't see her subjecting even a creep like Russ Buchanan to the hell she went through when Maya disappeared."

"She might if she thought she was saving Kylie's life."

Even as Thea formulated another argument, Reggie's words echoed at the back of her mind. *Bad men do bad things and get away with it all the time.*

She glanced up. "What is it you want me to do, Jake?"

"Nothing overt. Keep your eyes and ears open."

"Spy on my mother, you mean." Thea took a breath, suddenly so weary she could hardly hold up her head. His request distressed her in a way she couldn't explain. It prodded at all her old doubts. Dragged too many memories out into the open. Why had she ever thought coming back here a good idea?

The answer to that question was simple. This wasn't about her. This was about a missing child. In the world she and Jake had chosen for themselves, nothing else could ever be allowed to matter.

"I'll do what I can, but Reggie's injuries are serious. I have to be careful," she said.

"Of course. I would never ask you to do anything to impede her recovery."

She brought her eyes back to his. Their earlier camaraderie had vanished. The walls were up again and, everything considered, maybe that was a good thing. "Why do I get the feeling you've something else on your mind?" Her voice sounded stilted and slightly accusatory.

He returned her scrutiny for a moment then wordlessly took out his phone and slid it across the table.

Thea tore her gaze from his and picked up the phone. Goose bumps prickled as she studied the primitive figures then enlarged the image to bring the grotesque faces into focus.

"Have you ever come across anything like that?" Jake asked with a strange note of dread in his voice.

"Looks like some kind of talisman or totem," she said. "Not like any voodoo doll I've ever seen. Maybe Santeria, but I'd guess more Appalachian in origin. Or the Sea Islands, maybe. Seems like something that might be used in folk magic." She swiped and enlarged, bringing various parts of the figures into focus. "Where did this photo come from?"

"I took it. I found them hanging from a tree limb behind Reggie's house. Someone must have put them there after the initial canvass."

Thea couldn't tear her attention from the screen. "Where are they now? I'd like to see them in person."

"I've sent them to the lab for analysis."

She swiped again. "Do you think that's real human hair?"

"We'll know soon enough. I asked for priority."

She said slowly, "Maya had blond hair."

"So does Kylie Buchanan."

"And you found them behind Reggie's house? Where exactly?"

"Three or four hundred yards into the woods and directly over the path. I don't see how they could have been missed during any of the searches."

"Do you think they were put there as a way to connect the two missing girls?"

"That would seem the logical conclusion."

Thea studied the image a moment longer before handing back his phone. "Can you send that photo to me? I'd like to run it by someone. She's had some experience with occult-related abductions."

"Your number is the same?" When she nodded, he texted the image and then pocketed his phone. "You'll get back to me if you find out anything?"

"Of course." She pushed away from the table and stood. "I'm willing to help in any way I can, but right now I need to go and check on Reggie."

Jake stood, too. They walked out into the corridor and paused to say their goodbyes. He seemed hesitant to leave her alone. Sliding his hands in his pockets, he gazed down at her. "It's been a long time."

It was crazy how emotional she felt all of a sudden. "Yes, it has."

"I'm glad you're here, Thea." He turned and walked away, and this time she was glad he didn't look back. She brushed her hand against the wetness on her lashes and went to find her mother.

Chapter Four

Thea sat with Reggie for the rest of the afternoon and into the early evening. Still under the effects of anesthesia, her mother drifted in and out of sleep, rousing briefly to eat a few bites of Jell-O before falling back under. After the dinner tray had been collected and the doctor had come by, Thea gathered up her things and left.

One of the patrol officers at the crash site had rescued her backpack and carry-on from the trunk of her mother's car before it had been towed. As a courtesy, he'd promised to see that the bags were delivered to the Magnolia Hotel in downtown Black Creek where she had a reservation. Thea had murmured her gratitude as she'd climbed into the ambulance and then promptly forgotten about the luggage, though she'd kept the crossbody bag with her gun and ID close to her side. She hadn't given the rest of her things another thought until this very moment when the prospect of a hot shower and change of clothing had become irresistible.

She considered calling for a cab or car service, but the hotel was only a few blocks away and, despite the stiffness that dogged her every movement, she decided some fresh air would do her good.

Traffic was brisk in and out of the hospital parking lot, but the noise on the streets had already started to fade. It was that time of evening when daylight lingered and twilight hovered, and Thea's senses heightened. She could smell the jasmine that spilled over walls and fences, and the faint, dusty fragrance of the oleanders that lined the esplanade.

She left the main thoroughfare and turned down Market Street. Black Creek was modestly famous for its multitude of flea markets and antique shops that lined several blocks. Many of the stores had been in business since Thea was a little girl, but a few start-ups were sprinkled in among the originals. The passage of time struck her anew as nostalgia drifted in on the breeze and dread deepened with the shadows. She thought of Maya and little Kylie Buchanan and all the other missing children that had passed through her life since she'd left Black Creek. She thought of Reggie and the wedge that had been irrevocably driven between them after her sister's disappearance.

She tried not to think about Jake at all, but how could she not when she'd responded so viscerally to the sight of him? When, in a moment of fear, she'd reached instinctively for his hand to bolster her courage?

Her reaction had taken her by surprise, but how on earth had she not seen it coming?

It's over, she reminded herself. *It's been over for a long time. Don't even think about the possibility of going back there.*

They were too alike, she and Jake, and that had become an insurmountable obstacle. They each had things in their pasts they didn't want to talk about. Dark things that had turned both of them into scarred, wary loners.

The Magnolia Hotel was straight ahead. Shrugging off the melancholy, Thea crossed the intersection and entered the lobby. The desk clerk informed her that her bags had already been delivered to her room on the third floor. One of the perks of living in a small town, Thea decided as she thanked him, collected the key card and went straight up, barely taking the time to appreciate the artwork and antiques that decorated the careworn lobby.

The pair of queen-size beds in her room looked so inviting and Thea felt so worn out that she was tempted to shed her stained clothes and crawl under the covers right then and there. Instead, she went into the bathroom and turned on the tap. While the water heated, she stripped.

Plugging the drain, she climbed into the tub and lay back, letting the hot water soak away some of the aches and pains from the crash. She drifted off and when she startled awake, she had the strangest feeling that she was no longer alone.

She lay completely still in the tepid water, her senses attuned to the gloom outside the bathroom. She hadn't turned on any lamps in the bedroom and twilight had segued into night while she'd been soaking. Tilting her head, she tried not to splash as she peered out into the tiny hallway.

Nothing seemed amiss, but something was most definitely amiss. She could tell by the feathery warning at the back of her neck and another at the base of her spine. Her cross-body bag was on one of the beds where she had left it when she first walked in. She glanced around, taking stock of anything useful in the bathroom, and then eased up out of the water.

As she stepped over the side of the tub and reached for a towel, her heel came down on something sharp enough to pierce the skin. She muffled an exclamation as she sat on the edge of the tub and pulled a shard of glass from her foot. She thought at first it was a fragment from Reggie's shattered windshield that had clung to her hair or clothing. But rather than a chunky piece of safety glass, the sliver was thin and razor-sharp. Someone had broken a glass on the tiled floor, most likely.

Blood oozed from the tiny puncture. Thea grabbed a tissue and pressed it to the wound as she kept her attention focused on the bathroom door. Where there was one piece of glass, there were likely others, but she couldn't worry about that at the moment. She got up from the tub slowly and shrugged into her robe then hobbled out into the corridor.

A faint breeze drifted through the bedroom, raising goose bumps on her damp skin. She suddenly felt woozy and disoriented, which was odd. She'd never been squeamish at the sight of blood and the cut wasn't deep enough to put her in shock.

She tried to steady herself as she took a quick perusal of the room before removing her gun from the bag. Clutching the weapon in both hands, she scanned all the corners. The window that looked out onto the fire escape was open. Had it been open when she'd entered the room? She didn't think so, but she couldn't be sure. Exhaustion had dulled her senses. Just in case, she kept an eye on the opening as she backed into the corridor and checked the closet.

Satisfied she was alone, she returned the firearm to her bag and limped over to close the window. Her every move seemed slow-moving, heavy, and the room seemed to spin around her.

A car passed below and as the engine noise faded, Thea detected a melodic sound that seemed to reverberate across her nerve endings. The hollow clacking was strangely enticing and dangerously hypnotic. She slid the window all the way up and climbed out onto the metal landing, swaying precariously as she grabbed for a handhold.

Suspended from the fourth-floor landing, a pair of twig figures like the ones in Jake's photo hung down over her head. Their movement as they danced together in the breeze mesmerized her. Still slow motion, she put up a hand to touch them, except they dangled just beyond her reach. The shadows were deep on the landing. She could just make out tufts of blond hair and red fabric hearts. Or was she imagining them? Were the figures really there?

Everything seemed trippy, surreal. The streetlights below became elongated and so brilliant Thea had to glance away. The metal landing tilted beneath her and she dropped to her knees with a gasp. Threading her fingers through the grid, she clung for dear life even as she realized she must be stuck in a dream. None of this could be real.

Had she been drugged? But…how? When?

No sooner had the thought occurred to Thea than she became captivated once again by the sound of the twig figures. She sat cross-legged on the landing and tilted her head. The hollow carvings danced happily together and the music they made was as sweet and lyrical as summer rain.

At some point, she heard footsteps on the metal rungs below her, but she was too beguiled by the figures to turn her head. She had the strongest sense that some-one watched her from the shadows, reveling in her en-trancement.

Something changed then. The twig figures bumped together in the breeze, creaking and clacking as they rotated. Now she could see their faces, those grotesque black holes for eyes and the hideous gaping mouths.

Heart pounding, she tore her eyes from the fren-zied figures and concentrated on the open window. She needed to get inside to her phone. Jake would come. He might already be nearby.

Rising again to her hands and knees, she wove her fingers through the metal grid to propel herself up the slanted landing. It seemed impossibly steep all of a sud-den. She didn't dare look down. Above her, the figures swayed even more frantically as they tried to recapture her attention. They were now clearly malevolent with their grasping twig arms and pulsing red hearts.

In some part of Thea's consciousness, she realized she was deep into a drug-induced hallucination, but the danger seemed so real. She tried to shut everything out as she pulled herself inch by inch toward that open window then somehow over the sill and into the safety of her bedroom. She lay sprawled on the floor, terrified and shivering as she summoned the energy to reach for the phone. *Too far.*

The last thing she remembered was the melodic clack of the twig figures stirring in the breeze and a shadowy face with dark eyes and a gaping mouth peering in at her through the window.

THEA OPENED HER eyes slowly, blinked a few times and then threw her arm over her face to deflect the sunlight that streamed in through the window. She lay on top of the covers in her bathrobe, with no memory whatsoever of having gone to bed the evening before.

She squeezed her eyes closed as vague images danced at the edges of her consciousness. She remembered boarding the plane and landing in Tallahassee. She remembered Reggie picking her up at the airport and the car crash on the way home.

The car crash.

Ah. That explained the soreness in her joints and the deep ache in her every muscle. Probably also explained the throb behind her eyelids and the unpleasant roil in her stomach. She struggled to recall subsequent events. The hospital. Jake. Her long walk from the hospital to the hotel.

The Magnolia Hotel.

That's where she was. It was all coming back to her now.

She lifted herself onto her elbows and gazed around the room. Her backpack and carry-on were on the other bed, along with her cross-body bag. Fighting a wave of nausea, she swung her legs over the bed and sat with her head in her hands before reaching for the bag to make sure everything was still there. Firearm, credentials, phone. All there. All good.

Whatever the cause for her disorientation, she seemed mostly okay. Her right heel was tender when she tried to put weight on it, but the pain only blended with her other aches. She sat on the edge of the bed and examined the bottom of her foot. The skin was red around a small puncture wound and stained with dried blood.

Hobbling into the bathroom, she brushed her teeth and rinsed the bad taste from her mouth. As she reached for a fresh towel, her gaze dropped to the tiny smears of blood on the tiled floor. Okay, something else was coming back to her now. A vague recollection of pricking her foot on a piece of glass embedded in the fibers of the bath mat. She checked for other fragments and then rolled up the mat and placed it under the vanity along with the damp towel she'd used the evening before. Limping out to the bedroom, she left a note for housekeeping about the broken glass and grabbed a pair of flip-flops from her carry-on to wear in the bathroom just in case.

After a hot shower, she felt much better. Not as disoriented and queasy, though her memory was still sketchy. She put a Band-Aid over the puncture wound, dressed comfortably in jeans and sneakers and went to find coffee. A line had formed outside the hotel restaurant downstairs. The influx of volunteers and law enforcement personnel had no doubt stressed the capacity of the tiny dining room. Thea didn't feel like waiting for a table so she left the hotel, placing a quick call to the hospital to check on Reggie as she crossed the street to walk in the shade.

The antique shop on the corner was called the Indigo Dollhouse. Thea remembered it well from her childhood, in particular the signature blue Victorian dollhouse the owner had kept on display in the large bay window. The shop had once held a particular allure for Thea because it had been forbidden. Reggie had never allowed her to go inside to admire the antique dolls for fear she'd break something they couldn't afford to pay for. *This is June's kind of place, not ours*, she would say with that faint look of contempt she always got when she spoke of Thea's grandmother.

On impulse, Thea went over to the window. The dark blue dollhouse with its turrets and towers and gingerbread trim was still on display. Still beautiful and grand, though perhaps not quite as grand or as large as Thea remembered. A woman dusting inside the shop noticed her through the window and waved. Thea waved back and started to move on, but the woman came hurrying out of the shop and called her name.

"Thea? Thea Lamb?"

The shopkeeper looked familiar, but her name remained elusive. Thea's silence was awkward and a little embarrassing, but the woman didn't seem to notice.

"I thought that was you!" she exclaimed. "My goodness, I never expected to see you outside my window. How many years has it been?" She prattled on while Thea desperately tried to recall her name. She looked to be Thea's age, early thirties with highlighted brown hair braided down her back and wide hazel eyes. She paused after a moment and gave a little chuckle. "Oh dear. You don't remember me, do you?"

The name came to Thea in the nick of time. "Grace. Grace Wilkerson."

The woman beamed as she held up her left hand, allowing the gold band to catch the light. "It's Bowden now."

"Bowden." Thea's brow wrinkled in concentration. "Why do I know that name?"

"My husband is the chief of police," she said proudly. "You've probably heard his name around town. Nash Bowden."

"Yes, I'm sure Reggie has mentioned him."

The woman's smile vanished. She touched Thea's arm in concern. To Thea's credit, she managed not to back away. "How is your mom? I heard what happened."

"Do you mean the wreck or the kidnapping?" Thea asked brusquely.

"Both." Grace dropped her hand as she gave a little shudder. "After everything she went through all those years ago and now to have a child taken from her home in exactly the same way as her own. I mean, what are the chances? I just can't imagine what she must be going through. What you both are going through with all the memories."

"It's a difficult time for everyone," Thea said. "But especially for Kylie Buchanan's family."

"Yes, of course. I didn't mean to discount their pain. My heart goes out to them. But I can't help remembering the way it was around here after Maya went missing. The awful things people said about Reggie. As if losing a child wasn't bad enough." Her eyes glittered with compassion. "I also remember how it was for you in school. Kids can be so cruel. I only wish I'd been more supportive."

"You ate with me in the cafeteria and you came to my house to play with me. That's more than a lot of kids were allowed to do," Thea said.

"I should have stood up for you," Grace insisted. "If the situation had been reversed, you would have gone to battle for me."

"Who knows what I would have done? It's all ancient history at this point."

She nodded sadly. "There's no going back, is there?"

"No." Thea glanced away. Why was she thinking about Jake all of a sudden and wondering what her life might have been like if the promotion had never come through and he'd remained in DC? Would they still be together? Doubtful. And why did it even matter? Grace Bowden was right. There was no going back. Ever.

Grace sighed as if intuiting Thea's twinge of regret. "Tell me about Reggie. How is she physically? A car wreck on top of everything else. That poor woman. Can she ever catch a break?"

"She'll be okay. I'm on my way to see her now," Thea said.

Grace frowned in concern. "Please tell me you aren't walking all the way to the hospital in this heat. Forgive me for saying so, but you look as if you might keel over at any moment."

"I'm fine," Thea said. "I just need to find some coffee."

"There's a new coffee bar on Decatur where the old comic book store used to be. I hear it's quite good, but that's several blocks out of your way." Grace touched Thea's arm again. "I just made a fresh pot. Come inside and have a cup with me."

"I couldn't possibly impose."

"It's no imposition. Please. I would love the company." She seemed naturally effusive; a caregiver personality who gained energy from her physical and emotional connections with others. If one believed in personality types. In Thea's experience, people were complicated and so much more than just one thing.

"I really should get to the hospital," she said.

"But you wanted coffee first," Grace reminded her. "Come inside. It'll give us a chance to catch up. It's just lucky I spotted you through the window. I'm usually not even here on Wednesdays. I only open the shop on weekends these days. Otherwise, it's by appointment only for collectors." The bells over the door chimed as she beckoned persistently.

"Is doll collecting still a thing?" Thea stepped over the threshold and let the cool air wash over her. She caught herself and added quickly, "I hope that didn't sound rude. I've always been fascinated by this shop."

"It's a valid question," Grace said. "Interest ebbs and flows, as with any collectible. The hard-core magpies will always be around. I do most of my business online through eBay, Etsy and a few other sites. I'm only open today because I have a dealer coming in to look at one of my pre-Civil War dolls."

"Wow, that's old." Thea glanced around curiously, taking in the old-fashioned display cases, half of them empty. The floorboards creaked as she moved inside and a fine layer of dust hung in the air despite Grace's earlier efforts. *So this is the Indigo Dollhouse.*

"Dolls have been around since at least the ancient Romans," Grace explained. "The oldest in my collection dates back to the seventeenth century. She's priceless, though everything does have a price," she added with a wry smile.

"Whatever happened to the lady that used to own the shop?" Thea asked. "Wasn't she a relative of yours?"

"Yes, my great-aunt. She died a while back."

"I'm sorry."

Grace acknowledged Thea's sympathy with a brief nod. "She was sick for a long time. Nash said she was ready to go. He was probably right, but I still miss her."

"I'm sure you do."

She seemed to lose her train of thought for a moment, then shook off the shadows and gave Thea a bright smile. "So what do you think? Does the shop look the way you remember it?"

"Oh, I've never been inside until now," Thea said. "Reggie would never allow it. She was afraid I'd break something."

"Well, that's too bad. Aunt Lillian always loved when children came in. She used to keep some dolls and a little tea set in the back room to keep them occupied while their mothers browsed the more expensive items. I'm surprised you never came in with your grandmother. She was one of Aunt Lillian's most ardent customers."

"My grandmother?"

"Mrs. Chapman." Grace bit her lip. "I hope I didn't touch a nerve. I remember now that you were never very close."

"You didn't touch a nerve. I'd forgotten she collected dolls. I was rarely at her house." In truth, Thea knew very little about June Chapman. Maybe that was another reason the Indigo Dollhouse had enthralled her. Gazing through the big bay window was like glimpsing a small corner of her grandmother's strange world. Thea suspected that might account in part for Reggie's disdain. *I swear she sometimes acts as if those things are real. That can't be healthy, living alone in that big old house with no company but the cleaning lady and those creepy old dolls.*

"Make yourself at home," Grace said warmly. "Look at whatever you like. I'll go pour the coffee."

Thea moved around the shop, gazing inside the display cases as another memory tugged. She'd been eight or nine the first time she'd ever visited her grandmother's home on Crescent Hill. At least, that was the first and last time she could remember. The house hadn't been a place for children with its polished wood floors and pristine white sofas. She couldn't recall now why Reggie had left her there. She must have been desperate if she'd called June for help.

Her grandmother had made her play on the sunporch all day and she'd kept a cool, wary eye on Thea from the open French doors. At some point, the doorbell rang and she'd disappeared into the foyer to answer it. The shadowy interior had beckoned to Thea. Too curious for her own good, she'd crept inside and padded down the hallway until she came to an open doorway. Inside was a collection of the most beautiful porcelain dolls she could ever imagine. Most of them were protected inside glass cabinets, but a few had been artfully arranged around the room in intriguing vignettes.

Thea had already outgrown her own dolls by then. She was more into her bike and the secondhand rollerblades Reggie had found at a yard sale, but that forbidden collection had drawn her inside the room as surely as a moth to flame. She'd gone straight to a doll in a rocking chair. The blond curls and blue eyes had reminded her of Maya. Thea had trailed her fingers along the satin gown in reverence, the picked-at scab on the side of her hand long forgotten until a bead of blood left a rusty smudge on the delicate lace collar. Her grandmother had been speechless with rage when she found Thea trying to scrub away the stain at the bathroom sink. She'd grabbed her arm and dragged her back out to the sunporch.

Do you have any idea what you've done? That doll was priceless. You've ruined her beyond repair.

I'm sorry, Grandma—

Never call me that. Do you hear me? I am not your grandmother and you are nothing more to me than a horrible mistake. An abomination spawned by my son's weakness and that awful woman's conniving. He'd still be alive if not for her.

Thea hadn't known the meaning of "abomination." She'd gone home and looked it up. *A scandal, eyesore and disgrace.*

She'd never told Reggie about the doll incident, but as far as she knew, neither of them had set foot inside her grandmother's house after that day.

"How do you take your coffee?" Grace called out.

"Black is fine," Thea said as she tried to shake off the memory, but the lingering images left her unsettled.

"Come on back when you're ready." Grace glanced up when Thea appeared in the doorway. "I made blueberry muffins for my client. I always go overboard when I bake, so there're plenty. I thought you looked as if you could use a little something more than coffee." She motioned for Thea to sit.

Thea pulled out one of the painted chairs and sat. The kitchenette also showed the wear and tear of decades. The appliances were old and the ceiling stained from a persistent leak. A child-sized table and chairs with a miniature tea set and two raggedy dolls had been relegated to a dark corner. The sad little tableau depressed Thea for some reason.

"You really shouldn't have gone to so much trouble," she said as she picked up her cup and sipped.

Grace watched her with an anxious smile. "How is it?"

"Excellent. Hot and strong. Just the way I like it."

Her smile brightened. "Nash used to say he would have married me for my coffee alone."

"It's very good." Thea took another sip. "How long have you two been together?"

"We met during my senior year at Florida State. He was a police officer in Tallahassee. He ticketed me for speeding one day and then had the nerve to ask me to dinner that night. It was actually quite romantic." She smiled dreamily. "We were married six months later."

"What made you decide to come back to Black Creek?"

"My aunt got sick. I needed to come home and take care of her." She glanced across the table at Thea. "I don't know how much you remember about my family situation, but neither of my parents was all that reliable. They'd sometimes drop me off at my aunt's house and leave me there for days. God only knows what would have become of me without her. So I had to come back when she needed me."

"Of course," Thea murmured.

"Nash commuted for a while, but then he was offered the chief of police position here and we decided to relocate permanently. Despite what happened to your sister, Black Creek seemed like a good place to raise a family back then. Now I sometimes wonder if we'd been better off in Tallahassee. It's ironic, I suppose, that my husband came here because of me and now I stay because of him." Longing flickered across her features before she dispatched the melancholy with another quick smile.

You're hiding something, Thea thought. Aloud she said, "Relationships can be complicated."

"Yes, but enough about my boring life. Tell me about DC."

"How do you know I live in DC?" Thea asked.

A brow lifted. "Have you forgotten what it's like to live in a town this small? Everyone in Black Creek knows you work for the FBI. Isn't that why you're here? To help search for Kylie Buchanan?"

"Not officially. I came to be with Reggie. But, naturally, I'll help in any way I can."

"It's just so hard to believe something like this could happen again in our community. And the police don't seem to have any leads." She gazed at Thea expectantly over the rim of her cup.

"Your husband would know more about the case than I do," she said.

"Nash isn't one to bring his work home. I'm always the last to know anything."

"I'm sure you know as much as I do," Thea murmured in appeasement and wondered when she could politely excuse herself. She was starting to feel a bit claustrophobic in the tight space. Or maybe it was the hard edges behind Grace Bowden's too quick smile and the slightly bitter aftertaste of her coffee that made Thea suddenly apprehensive.

"Kylie and Taryn came in here once," Grace said.

Thea's mind had wandered, but now she snapped herself back to attention. "When was this?"

"A few weeks ago. I'd seen them around town now and then, but that was the first time they'd come into the shop. Kylie was like a beautiful little doll, so quiet and shy, you'd hardly even know she was there. I remember that Taryn seemed distracted. She kept glancing out the window. Her nervous behavior made me wonder about all the rumors I'd heard."

"What rumors?"

"That her husband was controlling and abusive. It was obvious she and Kylie were afraid of their shadows. I just wanted to wrap my arms around that sweet little girl and never let go."

"I can understand the impulse," Thea said. "How long were they here?"

Grace shrugged. "No more than ten minutes. After they left, they went down the street to the back entrance of the park. Kylie played on the swings while Taryn watched from the shade. After a while, a man came and sat beside her. I don't know why, but I had the impression they didn't want to be seen together."

Thea tried to picture the back entrance of the park in relation to the doll shop. Someone standing at the bay window would have to position herself just right to see all the way down the street and through the wrought-iron gate. Even then, she wasn't certain how much could be witnessed from that distance.

"You didn't recognize the man?" Thea asked.

"Oh, I did. He was Brother Eldon."

Eldon Mossey had been counseling Taryn since she'd left her husband, according to Thea's mother. Had the alleged clandestine meeting taken place before or after Taryn and Kylie had moved in with Reggie?

"You referred to him as Brother Eldon. I take it you go to his church?"

"Whenever I can. It's not always possible since I sometimes have appointments on Sunday."

"Did you ever see Kylie and Taryn at church?"

"A few times. Brother Eldon is quite the dynamic speaker. His sermons are so engrossing, I don't pay a lot of attention to the people around me."

Thea set aside her cup as she studied the woman's

expression. "Did you attend service on the Sunday night before Taryn went missing?"

The question seemed to disturb Grace. She closed her eyes briefly and nodded. "Yes. I saw Taryn playing on the new playground equipment before the service. I remember thinking how happy she looked compared to the shy, scared little girl I'd seen in my shop. Who could have known then what would happen to that sweet child in a matter of hours?"

"Did you stay for the whole service or did you leave early?"

Grace gave her a puzzled look. "Why would you ask that?"

"I just wondered if you'd seen Taryn and Kylie after the service."

"I don't think so. Not that I recall."

"Can you remember the exact day they came into the shop?"

"Why? Do you think it's important?"

"Probably not, but you never know."

Grace nodded. "I'll have to check my calendar and see if anything comes back to me. I'll do whatever I can to help."

"You didn't mention their visit to your husband?" Thea asked. "I'm surprised he didn't already have you check the date."

Her brow furrowed in concentration. "I don't know that I even thought about it until now."

"Have you ever met Russ Buchanan?" Thea asked, dropping any pretense that this was just a cordial reunion with an old school friend.

"Once, about a year ago. He came in looking for a birthday gift for Kylie. He was quite charming. A little too charming, if you know what I mean, but the rumors may have prejudiced my opinion." She got up and removed their plates. "Can I get you anything else?"

Thea took the hint and rose, too. "No, thanks. The coffee is excellent, but I need to be on my way."

Grace glanced over her shoulder as she stacked the plates in the sink. "It was good to catch up. I hope you'll stop by again if you get the chance."

"I'll try. Please do get back to me after you've checked your calendar." When Grace turned from the sink, Thea said, "You don't need to show me out."

Alone in the shop, she walked over to the bay window and glanced out. She could just make out the wrought-iron entrance to the back of the park, but no matter the angle, she couldn't glimpse inside the gate. Had Grace Bowden followed Taryn and Kylie to the park that day? Was that how she'd witnessed the clandestine meeting with Eldon Mossey? Maybe that was why she hadn't mentioned the incident to her husband. Her actions might be awkward to explain.

Thea started for the door, but an odd sound drew her around sharply. The melodic clacking was distant and elusive, like the tug of another old memory. She glanced around the faded shop as if the antique dolls in their dusty cases could somehow tell her what she needed to know.

Turning, she retraced her steps to the back room. Grace stood at the open door, staring out into a shady courtyard.

"What's that sound?" Thea asked.

The woman must have been deep in thought because she started and whirled, her hand flying to her heart.

"I'm sorry. I didn't mean to startle you," Thea said. "I'm curious about that sound."

Grace looked perplexed. "What sound? The dripping faucet? It's annoying, isn't it? I really need to call a plumber and get that thing fixed."

"No, not the faucet. That hollow, lyrical sound."

"Oh, you must mean my aunt's wind chime."

Thea stopped to listen. "That doesn't sound like any wind chime I've ever heard."

"No, it's wooden, but not like the cheap bamboo ones you see in discount stores. It was hand-carved by a local artisan. My aunt hung it in her white fringe tree for luck. Each chime has a distinct note. That's why the sound is so unusual." Grace stepped into the courtyard. "Sometimes, if the wind blows just right, it sounds like rain."

Like rain.

Something nudged at Thea's subconscious. A memory or an image that couldn't quite break free.

She followed the woman outside. The courtyard was cool and fragrant, a peaceful refuge from the noise of the busy street, yet Thea's disquiet deepened.

"Is this the sound you mean?" Grace went to stand beneath an ornamental tree, rippling her fingers through the wooden chimes that hung in varying lengths from one of the branches.

The hollow tubes were intricately carved with flowers and vines. No gaping mouths and eyes. Still, the hair prickled at the back of Thea's neck as she lifted her gaze. The Magnolia Hotel was just across the street. She could see the upper stories above the courtyard wall. It wasn't hard to pick out her room at the corner of the third floor and the window that opened onto the metal fire escape.

Was it possible she'd heard the wind chimes in her sleep last night? Had the hollow sound triggered bizarre dreams about the twig figures from Jake's photograph?

She turned to find Grace Bowden starring at her.

"Is something wrong?" Thea asked.

The woman smiled enigmatically as she rippled her fingers through the chimes. "I just love this sound."

Chapter Five

Jake was seated behind a table in the room Chief Bowden had designated for the FBI when he spotted Thea through the glass partition. She'd just come into the station and had stopped to show her badge and credentials to the uniformed officer at the front counter. The squad room was nearly empty. Most of the department was either on patrol, attached to a search party or assigned to one of the traffic stops. Jake saw her glance around curiously before the officer pointed her toward the back. She walked with a slight limp as she made her way through the maze of desks and cubicles. He got up and waited for her at the door.

"Thanks for coming," he greeted her.

She answered with a brief nod. "Of course. You said in your text you needed to see me as soon as possible." She took in his space with a glance. "Where's the rest of your team?"

"We had to set up a new command center at the courthouse. We ran out of space here. Most of the agents are either there or in the field. I haven't made the transition yet."

"You always did work best alone."

"Not anymore. I like to think I've become a team player."

"I suppose you have to be when you're in charge." Her gaze met his. Was that another note of censure he heard? A flicker of disappointment he detected in her eyes? Surely she didn't begrudge him his promotion and relocation. Because that would mean she still cared.

"I've learned to make the necessary adjustments," he said.

"Haven't we all?" She seemed to dismiss their past with a shrug. "So, what's up? I noticed a strange vibe when I came in just now. The officer at the front desk seemed on edge. You have news?"

"Nothing concrete and nothing good," he said then quickly added, "We haven't found Kylie."

"But there's been a break in the case?"

"Have a seat." He went around and took his place behind the laptop, closing the screen. "You want some coffee?"

She pulled out a chair and sat. "I just had coffee with the police chief's wife."

"I didn't know he was married," Jake said.

"I'm not surprised. You don't like small talk any more than I do."

"Then I'm going to surprise you by asking how you are."

She gave him a reluctant smile. "That's not really small talk, considering what happened yesterday."

"No, I guess it's not." He trailed his eyes over her features. Her skin looked pale in the artificial lighting and as fragile as parchment beneath the cuts and bruises. "Seriously, are you okay? You don't look so good."

His blunt assessment didn't seem to faze her. "I had a rough night. I think I dreamed about those weird twig things you showed me yesterday. And I kept hearing an odd sound all night. That sound is probably what triggered the nightmares."

"What kind of sound?"

"Hard to explain. Hollow and melodic is the best way I can describe it, but I know that won't make a lot of sense."

"It makes more sense than you know," Jake said. "That's the sound I heard in the woods yesterday before I discovered the figures hanging from a tree branch."

She stared at him. "That's a disturbing coincidence."

"Yes, it is."

"But I think I can explain the sound I heard," she quickly added. "There's a set of wooden wind chimes in the courtyard across the street from the hotel. My room looks down on it. The sound must have drifted up to me in my sleep."

"Do you know who owns the courtyard?"

"Yes. Grace Bowden. I saw the chimes myself before I came here. They look nothing like the figures you found."

Probably nothing to worry about, Jake decided, but he made a note to check out the chimes for himself. "It still seems a little coincidental that you would hear that particular sound in your sleep."

"Maybe. But it was a strange night all the way around," she said. "This morning I woke up queasy and disoriented. It took me a moment to even remember where I was." She paused. "If I didn't know better, I'd think I was drugged."

His voice sharpened in alarm. "Drugged? Where did you go last night?"

"Nowhere. I was with Reggie all afternoon until early evening. I left the hospital around eight and walked straight to the hotel, went up to my room, took a bath and then..." Her brow furrowed as she thought back. "Everything gets hazy after that. But memory loss isn't unusual under the circumstances. Car wrecks are stressful. People sometimes feel shock for days. I'm no exception."

"Shock could certainly explain the nightmares and the confusion," he agreed. "But it wouldn't hurt to see a doctor and get checked out."

"I was examined in the ER yesterday. I'll be fine in a day or two. I wouldn't have said anything, but I know how perceptive you can be. It was only a matter of time before you picked up on something. Then you would have weaseled it out of me one way or another."

He smiled. "If only it were that easy. I'm just glad you're okay. And Reggie? How's she doing?"

"She sounded surprisingly strong when I spoke to her earlier. She said she had a restful night."

"That's good to hear." He gave her another long scrutiny before dropping his regard.

"Jake." She leaned forward. "Are you going to tell me what's going on or not?"

"The police found the truck we think was involved in the hit-and-run. It was abandoned on a dirt road a few miles from the crash site. The vehicle had been torched, so no fingerprints or DNA, but we were able to recover the VIN number. The truck was reported stolen from a campsite near Lake Seminole a few days ago. It's possible the driver panicked after he hit you. He knew the highway patrol would be looking for the vehicle, so that's why he burned it."

"That doesn't explain why he followed us from the interstate and maintained the same distance until Reggie sped up," Thea said.

Jake picked up a pen and toyed with the cap. "Can you think of anyone who might harbor a grudge against Reggie?"

She didn't seem particularly surprised by the question. "As you noted yesterday, emotions run high in this town, especially when it comes to my mother."

"I'm not talking about gossip or even suspicions. I mean someone who has an actual vendetta."

His grim tone seemed to give her pause. "No one comes to mind. She and my paternal grandmother have never gotten along, but June is getting on up there in years. Back in the day, she could harbor a petty grudge for decades, but acting on a vendetta at her age? Just to be clear, that is what you're getting at, right? That someone deliberately ran us off the road to get even with Reggie? You must also think the driver is somehow connected to Kylie's disappearance. Why else involve yourself in a hit-and-run investigation?"

"It's a possibility on both counts," he said. "For the record, I don't see your grandmother being involved in either incident."

"Then who?"

"Do you remember a man named Derrick Sway?"

The name seemed to jolt her. She returned his scrutiny, her eyes narrowed and slightly accusing. "What does Derrick Sway have to do with Kylie Buchanan's abduction?"

"Just answer the question, please. Do you remember Derrick Sway or don't you?"

"Of course, I remember him. He was Reggie's boyfriend at the time of Maya's disappearance. The police hauled him in for questioning any number of times, from what I later read, but they never found anything to connect him to the kidnapping."

"What can you tell me about his relationship with Reggie?"

"I was only four years old at the time. You're asking a lot."

"I realize that."

She tucked back her hair, taking a moment to think about her response. "I don't know how helpful I can be. I have vivid memories about the night Maya disappeared, but I'd be surprised if even half of what I remember is real. It's possible—probable, even—that I've used everything I read and heard over the years to embellish a few vague images and impressions. For a time, I devoured everything I could get my hands on about the abduction."

"That's understandable," Jake said. "You never wanted to talk about it when we were together."

When we were together.

Their gazes clung for a moment before Thea glanced

away. Did she remember, as he did, all those lazy Sunday mornings in bed, with their phones silenced and their coffee cooling on the nightstands? Something glimmered in her eyes that told him she did remember. But maybe that was only wishful thinking. His way of embellishing a delusion.

"It's still hard for me to talk about," she said. "Maya and I weren't identical twins but we looked a lot alike and we had a very strong bond. 'Two peas in a pod,' Reggie used to say. On the night she went missing, Maya climbed into my bed because she heard a dog baying in the woods and it scared her. I was hot so after she went to sleep, I moved over to her bed."

"You never told me that." Jake got up and walked around the table, leaning against the edge as he folded his arms and looked down at her.

"If I'd stayed in my own bed, maybe I would have been taken instead of Maya. Twenty-eight years later, I still wonder about that."

"Thea…"

Don't, her eyes seemed to plead. *Don't look at me that way.* As if he had the power *not* to look at her that way.

She cleared her throat. "Anyway, you were asking about Derrick Sway's relationship with my mother. They used to argue, sometimes loudly, but I never saw him lay a hand on her."

"How did he treat you and Maya?"

"He mostly ignored us. If he'd ever gotten physical, Reggie would have kicked him out. She had a lot of faults, but she wasn't shy about defending herself or her kids."

"Maybe she didn't know."

"If he'd done anything bad to us, I would remember," Thea insisted.

"That's not necessarily true," Jake said gently. "You know as well as I do that children often block traumatic memories."

"And yet I'm able to recall that howling dog as clearly as if it were yesterday."

"Isn't it possible—"

"No. Maya and I were inseparable back then. I would have known if he'd hurt her."

Jake didn't try to push the issue any further. "Did you know that Sway was in prison for ten years?"

"Reggie mentioned it once."

"Do you remember what she said about it?"

"Just that he finally got what was coming to him."

"That's a pretty powerful statement. What do you think she meant by that?" he asked in that same gentle tone.

"He was a thief and a drug dealer. I imagine that's what she meant."

"Did she suspect he had something to do with Maya's disappearance?"

"She never let on if she did."

"But they parted on bad terms."

"Relationships end for all kinds of reasons. Maybe she finally saw him for who he really was." Thea seemed to grow weary of the conversation. Or maybe she didn't like him poking around in her past. She was a private person who'd experienced tragedy at a young age. He hated stirring up all her old memories, but she'd be the first to agree that nothing could be off limits when a child's life was at stake.

She got up and walked over to the glass partition, studying the deserted squad room before turning to face him. "Reggie changed after Maya's disappearance. She stopped drinking and smoking, and started experimenting with religion."

"'Experimenting'? That's an odd way of putting it."

"Not if you knew Reggie."

"Do you know if she and Sway kept in touch?"

"I doubt it. When Reggie was done, she was done."

Like mother, like daughter, Jake thought.

Thea sighed. "This is getting very tedious. Why all the questions about Reggie and Derrick Sway? I think I deserve an explanation. It's obvious you regard him as a suspect, but why? You must have something more than an abandoned truck and a gut feeling to go on."

"He was released from prison several months ago. The last known address we have for him is his mother's home in Yulee. A police officer went by there yesterday afternoon, but Sway was nowhere to be found. His mother claims she hasn't seen him in weeks."

"That doesn't answer my question. Is he a suspect or isn't he?"

"Right now, he's certainly a person of interest."

"Why?" she demanded. "Stop beating around the bush and tell me what you have on him."

"There was a possible sighting of him a few weeks ago at Lake Seminole."

"Where the truck was stolen," Thea said. "What else?"

Now Jake was the one who considered his answer carefully. "Sway may be under the impression that Reggie was the one who turned him in to the police. If so, he could blame her for his incarceration."

Thea came back over to the table. "That's a very big if, isn't it? How would abducting Kylie Buchanan give him payback? Unless he thinks he can make Reggie relive Maya's disappearance. Or somehow frame her for the kidnapping."

"There may be an even darker motive," Jake said. "A neighbor said he mistook Taryn for you when he first noticed her and Kylie living at Reggie's house. He assumed Kylie was your daughter."

That seemed to take her aback.

"It's an understandable mistake from a distance," Jake said. "Especially if he hasn't seen you in years. You and Taryn have a similar build and coloring. Both blond. Both trim and fit. If Sway made the same assumption about Taryn and Kylie as the neighbor, he could have taken Kylie because he thought she was your daughter. Reggie's granddaughter."

Thea let out a breath. "My God. That's a chilling thought."

"It is."

She bit her lip as she contemplated the implications. "It still seems like a reach to me."

"I thought so, too, until the officer went to talk to his mother. He said the woman seemed scared to death of Sway. He was always trouble, according to her, but she hardly recognized him when he got out of prison. He was into some very disturbing things, apparently."

"Like 'making hideous twig dolls and hanging them in a tree behind my mother's house' kind of disturbing?"

"Mrs. Sway wouldn't elaborate, only that after he moved in, strangers started showing up at the house at all hours. She didn't know what they were up to, but she called them evil."

"Could she identify any of these people?"

"Unfortunately, no. She said they always stayed outside in the dark or came in through the back door, like they didn't want to be seen. If she questioned Derrick about what he was up to, he'd burn something in his bedroom to make her think he was setting the house on fire."

"That's sadistic."

"*Sadistic* would be a good word to describe his behavior, according to his mother."

"Where is he now?"

"She swears she doesn't know. She said he got a phone call a few weeks ago and took off in the middle of the night. She hasn't seen or heard from him since. But she did allow the officer inside to look through his room." Jake reached across the table for an evidence bag. "Most of his things had been cleared out, but the officer found this slid behind the baseboard in the closet."

Thea's face went even paler as she stared at the photograph in the bag. "This was found in his possession?"

"In his room, yes. Do you recognize it?" Jake asked.

She closed her eyes. "It's a snapshot of Maya standing on our front porch. It was taken on our fourth birthday, just a couple of months before she went missing. Reggie used to keep that photograph on the refrigerator where she could see it every morning when she had her coffee. Then one day she boxed up all the photographs and put them away in her closet. Maybe that was the day both of us gave up on Maya ever coming home."

"How long ago did you last see this photograph?"

He saw her take a deep breath as she thought back. "I don't know. I was still a kid. Maybe ten or eleven when she put everything away."

Maya had been taken when she was four years old. That was a long time to wait for a sister to come home. "The photo has been torn in two."

"So I noticed."

"The raw edge looks like it's been singed." Jake paused. "Were you in the other half of the photograph?"

"Yes." She couldn't seem to tear her eyes from her sister's image. "You can tell from the position of Maya's arm that we were holding hands. We always did when Mama took our picture."

Jake had never heard her call her mother anything but Reggie. She had a soft, faraway look in her eyes, as if she'd slipped back in time. He wanted to reach over and take her hand, to tell her everything would be okay, but the present-day Thea knew better. "How do you think Sway came to be in possession of this photograph?"

"I have no idea. There's no way Reggie would have ever given it to him. He must have come into her house and stolen it at some point or else there were two similar photographs and he took one when he left."

"Why would he do that? You said he showed no particular interest in you and Maya. He ignored you. Why tear you out of the photograph? Why keep an image of your sister all these years?"

"It makes me sick to my stomach to even contemplate." She handed him back the bag. "You think he took her, don't you? Maya, I mean."

"You said yourself the police never found anything to connect him to her disappearance. Even so, I don't think we can discount the possibility."

She was visibly shaken but trying desperately to cling to her composure. "What can I do to help?"

"You've already done your part. You've answered all my questions. Now the best thing for you to do is to go be with your mother at the hospital."

"Just like that. No further need of my services."

Jake gave her a soft smile. "You know that's not what I mean. We've got people actively searching for Derrick Sway. Every law enforcement body in the state is on alert. I'll let you know as soon as I hear anything. You have my word."

"I guess that will have to be enough."

He placed the evidence bag on the table and turned back to her. "I know I don't have to tell you this, but please be careful. Even Sway's own mother is terrified of him."

"The torn photograph seems to indicate he has no interest in me," she said.

"Or maybe it indicates the exact opposite. If he abducted Kylie out of mistaken identity, he's probably been following the news and is aware of who she is by now. If he's out for revenge against Reggie, his desire for payback won't have been satisfied. In fact, he may be even more determined. Reggie should be safe enough in the hospital. Sway won't show his face in public. He'd be too easily recognized. But you need to watch your back."

"I'm not concerned for my own safety," Thea said. "What if your theory is true? What happens to Kylie if Sway took her by mistake?"

Jake said nothing for a moment. He didn't have to.

"All we can do is stay focused and keep looking."

"Why do I get the feeling you're holding something back?"

He ran a hand across his eyes. "It's nothing tangible. Even with this new lead, I can't help thinking we're missing something hidden in plain sight. Something darker than any of us has imagined." He gave her a worried look. "I can't explain it, but I can feel it."

Chapter Six

Thea felt drained after her conversation with Jake, which wasn't surprising. She'd prepared herself for an emotional roller-coaster ride when she'd made the decision to come to Black Creek. The similarities in Maya's and Kylie's abductions were bound to stir old memories. She'd spent a lifetime building up her defenses, but the news about Derrick Sway combined with the lingering shock from the car crash had left her temporarily vulnerable. Physically, she was nowhere near a hundred percent, so when Jake had offered her a ride to the hospital, she'd gratefully accepted. Why push herself beyond her limit just to prove she could get there on her own steam?

She waited for him outside in the shade of the building, relieved to have a moment alone to regroup. She wanted to believe he'd been forthcoming about Derrick Sway and what they'd found at his mother's house, but something was always held back from the public. Since she had no official standing in the investigation, she couldn't expect to be read in on every new development, but how could she protect herself—let alone Reggie—if she wasn't given the whole picture?

A day ago, she might have dismissed his mistaken identity theory out of hand, but something strange had happened to her last night. She could explain away the nightmares and disorientation, but what about the doubts that niggled at the back of her mind? What about those vague images that drifted at the fringes of her memory?

What if Derrick Sway had been creeping around on the fire escape last night?

What if he'd slipped through the window while she'd been soaking in the bathtub or sleeping in her bed?

Thea shivered despite the heat. That torn photograph was the first lead they'd had in her sister's case in twenty-eight years, not to mention the first concrete link to Sway. Little wonder she felt blindsided by Jake's revelation. The notion that Maya's abductor had still been around all these years, that he might even have kept a picture of her with him in prison, sickened Thea to her very core.

What had he done with the other half of that photograph? Had Thea's image been tossed in the trash years ago or did Sway have another purpose for her in mind?

For a dizzying moment, she thought she might have to vomit in the grass. She sucked in air and tried to focus. The faintness subsided, but her fears only grew stronger. Jake was right. Something very dark pulsed beneath the surface of this town. Two children had gone missing from her mother's home. Maya was lost forever, but Kylie Buchanan still had a fighting chance.

Three percent, Thea thought fiercely.

No way could she sit idly by at the hospital while another child was in danger, perhaps from the same monster that had taken her sister. Reggie was safe for now. She didn't need a daughter she barely knew hovering over her. Thea's time would be better spent out searching for Kylie Buchanan. Jake was the best at what he did, but Thea wasn't without experience and insight. She knew the town and she knew the people. She knew things he didn't. *Go back to the beginning. Go back to the place where Kylie and Maya were taken.*

The roar of a car engine drew her attention to the street. She thought at first Jake had brought his vehicle around to pick her up, but instead a silver Mercedes wheeled to the curb in front of the police station. A tall man in his late thirties got out and strode toward the front steps, pausing on the bottom stair when he caught sight of Thea in the shade. A look of bemusement swept over his features. He stepped back down on the sidewalk.

"Excuse me, miss. Are you okay?"

"Yes, I'm fine, thank you." She glanced at the street. "I'm waiting for my ride."

He hesitated. "I know this may sound trite, but have we met?"

"I don't think so," Thea said, although she'd quickly deduced who he was from the make and color of his car. Even on such a hot day, Russ Buchanan was sharply dressed in a gray suit and crisp white shirt. He was tall, trim, and Thea supposed he was handsome if one could ignore his imperious demeanor.

"Wait a minute. I know who you are," he said in a low drawl. "I can see the resemblance now. You're Reggie Lamb's daughter."

"Thea," she said with a nod.

"The FBI agent. I heard you were in town. I'm Russ Buchanan." He moved off the sidewalk and approached her in the shade. Thea couldn't help noticing that every lock of his dark wavy hair lay perfectly in place and that even with a few feet between them she could catch a whiff now and then of something understated and expensive.

She gave him a subtle assessment as she offered her sympathy. "I'm very sorry for what you're going through, Mr. Buchanan. My family has been where you are. If there's anything I can do—"

He cut her off. "Do you mean that?" His tone was genial, but the eyes that locked onto hers were cold and empty. Or was she letting the accounts of his abuse color her first impression of him?

Thea tried to tamp down her prejudgment. "Yes, of course I mean it."

He set his jaw as the cordiality drained from his voice and he took a step toward her. "Then you tell that hag of a mother of yours to stay the hell away from my wife."

And there it was. The underlying threat of violence. The impervious disregard for anyone else's feelings or welfare. So much for giving him the benefit of the doubt.

Thea stared into those soulless eyes without flinching. "Surely that's a decision your wife can make for herself."

"The last time she made a decision for herself, my daughter ended up missing. Taryn is now learning the hard way that actions have consequences."

Thea's gaze narrowed slightly. What did he mean by that? Aloud, she said, "I understand the need to blame someone—"

"Oh, I know exactly who to blame," he assured her. "Let me put it to you this way. If anything happens to my little girl, Reggie Lamb will wish she'd gone to prison twenty-eight years ago when she murdered her own kid."

Thea kept her expression neutral as anger and dread battled inside her. The worst thing she could do was let a sociopath like Russ Buchanan believe he'd gotten under her skin. He obviously intended to provoke a confrontation, maybe create an unpleasant scene in front of the police station that he could somehow use against Reggie.

"Are you threatening my mother, Mr. Buchanan?"

"I'm simply letting you know that I'm on to her. And for the record, I'm on to you, too. I know why you're here. If you think you can use your influence to steer the investigation away from Reggie, I would strongly suggest you reconsider."

"What are you talking about?"

He gave her an odd smirk before glancing up the steps to the police station. "I knew as soon as I heard you were in town it would only be a matter of time before you tried to insinuate yourself into the investigation. That's why I'm here, actually. To warn Chief

Bowden to block you from anything related to my daughter's case."

"The more people working to find your daughter, the better, I would think."

"Yes, you would think that. After all, it would be so much easier to destroy incriminating evidence if you were assigned to Kylie's case."

"I won't be assigned to Kylie's case," she told him. "But even if I were, I'd never destroy or compromise evidence regardless of who it incriminates."

"You say that now, but what happens if you suddenly find yourself standing between your own mother and prison?"

"You seem so certain of her guilt," Thea said. "Why is that, I wonder?"

"Her history speaks for itself."

"No. It's not that." She searched his face, letting a pensive note seep into her voice. "If I didn't know better, I'd think you're trying to deflect."

Another sneer flashed, along with a subtle gleam in his eyes that warned her she couldn't touch him. He was in full control.

We'll see about that.

"Reggie took your wife and child into her home when they had no place else to go. I think that's the real reason for your animosity," Thea said. "You resent her for giving Taryn and Kylie a way out."

His dark gaze flickered for the first time. He didn't like being reminded of his failure to keep his family in line. Thea couldn't get a read on his true feelings for

Kylie, but he made no attempt to disguise his utter disdain for the child's mother.

"Taryn is a sick woman," he said. "For as long as I've known her, she's been prone to depression and delusions, especially when she's off her medication. Your mother took advantage of her fragile mental state. She manipulated Taryn into believing that I was a danger to my own wife and child. Ironic—isn't it?—considering Reggie's past."

"She was never charged or convicted of anything," Thea reminded him.

"A box was dug up in the woods behind her house containing her daughter's DNA. That's right," he said as if interpreting Thea's surprise. "I know all about that box. I had Reggie Lamb thoroughly investigated the minute I found out Taryn had moved our daughter into her home. No matter how long ago it happened, people in this town remain unconvinced of your mother's innocence. Some of them believe she murdered your sister and buried her hastily in the woods. Then she went back later and moved the body. Maybe she threw her in a lake or dug a deeper hole somewhere more remote."

Thea suppressed another shiver. "That's quite a vivid picture you've painted."

He'd gone straight for the jugular, but now he softened his voice and demeanor as easily as a chameleon superficially changing its color. "I can only imagine how it must have been for you. Your twin sister, the person you were closest to in the whole world, abandoned to a cold, hidden grave by your own mother."

He was good. Thea would give him that. Even with

her experience and insight, she felt the pull of his devious accusations.

He canted his head. "I feel for you. I truly do. I can't imagine what it must have been like growing up in the house with that woman, feeling her lips against your cheek before you went to sleep. Hearing her footsteps in the middle of the night, knowing what you knew."

You creepy bastard.

He put out a hand in supplication. "Please understand. I have nothing against you personally, Agent Lamb. I wish you no ill will. In fact, I was very sorry to hear about your accident. Roads have become hazardous places these days. People become enraged over the slightest infraction."

"Sometimes for nothing more than a perceived infraction," Thea said. She waited a beat. "Do you own a black pickup, Mr. Buchanan?"

"What would I do with a pickup truck? Although I suppose they're useful for hauling things."

"You're a defense attorney, correct? A successful one, from what I hear. That gives you access to an extensive roster of criminal clients, some of whom might be persuaded to do any number of dirty deeds for the right price. I wonder if one of them owns a pickup. Or would be willing to steal one for you."

He shook his head sadly. "Such a wild imagination. It must be a burden in your line of work. If you're not careful, you might start to see and hear all sorts of strange things."

Like hollow dolls with twig limbs and gaping holes

for mouths and eyes? "Do you know an ex-con named Derrick Sway?"

"No, why? Is he someone important?" Was that a slight twitch at the corner of his mouth? The barest telltale flicker deep down in his cold, calculating eyes?

"If I were to dig into Derrick Sway's background, I wouldn't find your name on any of his court filings?"

"You bitch." He purposely let his mask slip, giving her another glimpse of the violence that simmered beneath the surface of his carefully refined façade. "You have no idea who you're dealing with."

"On the contrary," Thea said. "I know exactly who you are."

"Then you should be smart enough to keep your nose out of my business." He reached out as if to grab her arm, but the look on Thea's face stopped him cold.

"Or what?" she demanded. "You'll have someone run me off the road?"

He dropped his hand to his side and smiled. "You said it yourself. I have a whole cadre of criminal clients at my disposal. You'd be surprised at how creative and enthusiastic—not to mention, grateful—some of them can be."

"THAT DIDN'T APPEAR to be a friendly conversation," Jake observed when Thea climbed into his SUV.

"Anything but," she confirmed as she watched the silver Mercedes peel away from the curb and swerve into traffic, narrowly missing an oncoming vehicle. Evidently, he'd changed his mind about talking to the police chief, at least for now.

Jake swore under his breath. "Good way to get some-body killed. You must have really touched a nerve if he's driving like that in front of the police department."

Thea made a disgusted face. "He's under the impres-sion the police can't or won't touch him. He's actually pretty open about it. I wouldn't be surprised if he has a friend or two on the inside protecting him. They're probably also feeding him information about the inves-tigation. He certainly knew I was in town."

"I wouldn't read too much into that," Jake said. "Word gets around in a place like this. Half the town probably knows you're here by now." He glanced in the rearview mirror before merging with traffic.

"What's your take on Chief Bowden?"

He gave her a surprised look. "Seriously? You think the police chief is in Buchanan's pocket?"

"I'm just asking what you think of him."

Jake focused on the road. "He's a good cop. Dedi-cated and by the book. Mostly."

"Mostly?"

He gave her another look. "Come on. We both know no one is perfect. Liberties are sometimes taken when a child's life is in danger."

"Did you know he used to be with the Tallahassee Police Department? According to his wife, they moved down here so that she could take care of her ailing aunt. I got the impression from Grace that she would like to move back to the city, but she stays here because of her husband. I guess that makes me wonder about him."

"Why? Because he likes living and working in a small town? There's something to be said for getting out of the rat race." He stopped at a traffic light. Up ahead, the silver Mercedes sped through another intersection and disappeared.

"You wouldn't last a month in a backwater place like this," Thea scoffed. "Neither would I, for that matter."

"I can tell you this about Nash Bowden. He did everything right when he received the call about a missing child. He alerted the field office immediately so that CARD could be activated. Not a moment's hesitation over territory. He's also the one who initiated the door-to-door canvass and K-9 tracking. His quick response saved us hours of valuable time once we were on the scene."

"You like him," Thea said.

"I respect what I've seen of his work. I'd be very surprised if he could be bought off by anybody, let alone a man like Russ Buchanan."

Thea settled back against the seat as the light changed and they moved down the street. "I trust your judgment. It's just… I got a strange vibe from his wife this morning. Like she was hiding something. Like maybe things aren't so great in the Bowden marriage."

"How is that relevant?"

Thea shrugged. "Maybe it's not, but sometimes people do things out of character when money becomes a problem. Grace runs an antique doll shop she inherited from her aunt. You should see the place. It looks as if it hasn't been updated in fifty years and the display cases are half empty. She says she does most of her business online, so maybe that accounts for the lack of inventory in the shop. But how much of a living can someone make selling dolls?"

"Depends on how rare and valuable they are, I guess." He turned to give her a quick scrutiny. "What are you thinking? That the chief takes money under the table to pad their bank account? Or are you suggesting the Bowdens are somehow involved in Kylie Buchanan's abduction?"

"It sounds ridiculous when you say it out loud," she conceded. "It's possible I imagined the weirdness with Grace. She caught me off guard and God knows I'm not at my best at the moment. Still…"

"What is it?"

"Maybe you're not the only one who has a premonition," she said.

He frowned at the road. "I never called it that."

"Relax. It was a lame joke. But like you, I can't help feeling that we're missing something." When he didn't respond, she said his name softly. "Jake. You do know I was kidding, right?"

He gave her a lingering glance. "Yeah. Bad memories."

About what? Thea wondered. Bad memories from their time together or from his early years in foster care? He never talked much about those days. Neither of them had been willing to open up about their pasts, but she'd gleaned enough to know he'd had a tough childhood. Abused and abandoned by the time he was seven. No wonder he fought so hard for the children who went missing.

She thought about the scars on his back and the deeper wounds inside his soul. For all her faults, Reggie had never mistreated her children. She'd hardly ever raised her voice to them. Thea couldn't imagine what it must have been like to lay awake at night trying to intuit his tormentor's next move. Honing his senses to detect the slightest sound or motion and then scrambling under the bed or into the closet to escape a drunkard's inexplicable wrath.

Jake's brooding scowl tore at Thea's resolve. She resisted the urge to reach across the console and take his hand. Neither of them had ever believed in any kind of psychic phenomenon, but at times his instincts seemed uncanny. She would never try to label his insight any more than she would attempt to explain the feel of a child's hand against her cheek in the dead of night. The overwhelming certainty at times that Maya was near could be nothing more than wishful thinking, a sensation akin to the phantom ache of a missing limb.

"Are you okay?"

Jake's voice cut into her reverie. She sighed. "Bad memories like you said."

"You've had a rocky homecoming."

"Yes. Although it's hard to remember a time when I considered this place home."

He gave her a quick perusal. "You never told me why Russ Buchanan got so riled up earlier."

"I guess I pushed the wrong buttons. He had a definite agenda when he approached me. He insists Reggie is responsible for his daughter's disappearance, and he thinks if I'm involved in the investigation, I'll hide or destroy evidence that could incriminate her."

"We both know that's not true."

His certainty gratified her, but Thea couldn't quite turn off the little voice in her head that reminded her of the discrepancy she'd uncovered in Reggie's statement. She hadn't told anyone what she'd found, even Jake. Why make a mountain out of a molehill about an open window? But no matter how hard she tried to convince herself Reggie's omission was just an oversight or an innocent mistake, Thea had never quite put those doubts to rest.

She studied Jake's profile before turning to stare out at the passing shops. "I think Buchanan is the one who had us run off the road yesterday. He didn't outright admit it, of course. He's too smart for that. He said just enough to try to get under my skin."

"Did he succeed?"

"He's a narcissistic sociopath who beats his wife. What do you think?"

"You need to be careful with Buchanan," Jake warned. "Whether he has the local law in his pocket or not, he's the kind of guy who'd take satisfaction in causing as much trouble as he can for you and your mother."

"I didn't seek him out. He's the one who came to me. He said he wanted a word with the chief, but I wonder if someone tipped him off that I was at the station. In any case, I'm not afraid of a creep like Buchanan. Reggie certainly isn't," she added with a note of pride.

"Like mother, like daughter," Jake muttered.

"What?"

"Nothing. What else did he say?"

"I think he may know Derrick Sway. I'm pretty sure I detected a slight reaction when I mentioned Sway's name."

"Pretty sure?"

"I may not possess your keen powers of observation, but I have a strong suspicion there's a connection. I think Sway may be a former client."

"Ten years ago when Sway went to prison, Buchanan would have barely been out of law school," Jake pointed out.

"Which would have made him hungry for even a low-life client like Derrick Sway. It's also possible he came in later to handle an appeal or some other type of legal proceeding. I know it's a long shot, but so is your mistaken identity theory."

"I'll have it checked out," Jake promised. He shifted the blinker to merge into the right lane.

Thea sat up. "Wait. I've changed my mind about going to the hospital."

"Isn't your mother expecting you?"

"I'll give her a call and tell her I've been delayed. She'll understand."

His gaze turned suspicious. "What are you up to?"

"Nothing. I just want to spend some time in the house where I grew up."

"Why?"

"Because I want to see where Kylie was taken."

"Kylie or Maya?"

She swung around to face him. "Does it matter? If your theory is true, the same monster took both girls."

"It's too early to draw that conclusion," Jake cautioned.

"Maybe. But I know you're thinking it, too."

Ever since he'd shown her the torn photograph, Thea had felt compelled to return to her old house, to revisit the room she'd once shared with her twin sister. To spend time in the place where she'd felt closest to Maya. If she closed her eyes, she could almost feel the breeze from that open window…she could almost hear her sister's tremulous voice in the dark. *I'm scared, Sissy.*

"You don't have to stay," she said a few minutes later when Jake turned down Reggie's street.

He gave her a skeptical look. "You expect me to drop you off and leave you without any transportation?"

"Why not? I know my way around the area." But despite her familiarity with the surroundings, Thea was starting to get a surreal vibe from the neighborhood. She'd forgotten how old the houses were in this part of town, how the mature trees blocked all but slivers of sunlight in places. The lots were bigger on Reggie's side of the street. Rather than backing up to another row of houses, the yards ran right up against several acres of untouched woodland.

If you walked all the way through the trees, you came out near an opening in the rocks that led into one of the few known caves located outside the state park system. The locals had dubbed the entrance the Devil's Pit, a gross exaggeration since the initial descent was no more than fifteen or twenty feet. Most of the cave was dry, but an underground river ran beneath the structure, bubbling up into pools in some of the caverns. Thea had never gone down into even the first room. She wasn't claustrophobic, but the place frightened her. Years ago, two teenagers had become disoriented trying to find a way out; they'd drowned inside an underwater passageway. Now the whole landscape around the cave seemed heavy and oppressive. Or maybe she'd watched too many horror movies growing up.

"Has anyone searched the cave?" she asked.

"The local police sent a search party in with a guide early on. From what I understand, even some of the dry passageways are hard to navigate. They searched as far as they could go, but they didn't find anything."

"The locals didn't find those twig figures in the trees, either," Thea reminded him.

"I'll talk to Chief Bowden. Can't hurt to take another look." He pulled up in the driveway and cut the engine.

"You really don't have to stay," Thea said. "I know you're needed elsewhere."

He watched her for a moment as if trying to detect an ulterior motive. "You're not planning on going down in the cave alone, I hope."

She gave a slight shudder. "I wouldn't do that. I meant what I said. I want to spend some time in the house. I'll be fine. I'll call a cab when I'm ready to leave." Her attention strayed to the faint lettering at the side of porch. *Murderer.*

Memories assailed her as she moved her focus over the vandalized siding and up the porch steps to the place where the photograph of her and Maya had been taken. Their birthday dresses had been identical except for the color. Maya's pink and Thea's yellow.

She glanced at Jake. He stared almost trancelike out the windshield toward the backyard and the woods beyond. His utter stillness unnerved her.

"What is it?"

He gave a casual nod at the house. "You go on inside

and do what you need to do. While I'm here, I may as well take a walk back through the woods." He opened the door and got out.

Thea climbed out after him and came around the vehicle to confront him. "Why do I get the feeling you're the one who's up to something? You know I don't like it when you get all cryptic. What's going on in that head of yours?"

"Nothing. I won't be long."

Thea let out a frustrated breath. "I forgot how maddening it is when you get like this."

He turned with a frown. "I'm not being cryptic. If someone has been creeping around your mother's place, they may have left another clue."

"Are you sure that's all it is? You didn't see or hear something I should know about?"

"I didn't see or hear anything. I'm being straight with you. I'm here, so why not take another look?"

She tried another tact. "Maybe we shouldn't separate."

"I'll be fine."

He started to turn away but she caught his arm. "Call or text if you need me. You know I'll have your back, right?"

He nodded. "That's the one thing I've never had to worry about."

Chapter Seven

The woods were too quiet. Jake half expected to hear that strange hollow melody as he headed deeper into the trees, but nothing so much as a birdcall came to him. It was almost as if someone else moving through the woods ahead of him had scared all the wildlife away.

He wasn't anticipating trouble, but if he'd learned anything during his time as a federal agent, it was always best to prepare for the worst. His weapon was holstered, and he had his phone and a flashlight with him in case he decided to walk all the way to the cave. He had no intention of descending alone, but he could at least search the terrain around the entrance and shine his light inside the pit. If he saw anything suspicious, he'd call for backup. For now, he wasn't about to pull his team away from their current assignments to assist on a hunch that could end up a wild-goose chase.

He kept to the path, walking slowly but steadily as he searched tree branches and all through the underbrush, still uncertain of his objective. He hadn't seen or heard anything out of the ordinary. He'd had no bursts of insight, no strong compulsion to enter the woods like he'd experienced the day before. Just a persistent needle at the back of his neck that told him to keep walking. Keep looking. *Children don't disappear into thin air.*

Pausing on the path, he glanced over his shoulder. Sunlight glimmering down through the canopy created a strange surreal effect on the trail. For a moment, he could have sworn someone stood in the shadows, just beyond reach of the dappled light. His imagination, of course. His dazzled vision had conjured an image of Kylie's faceless abductor as he'd traveled through the woods that night, carrying the child in his arms. He'd probably subdued her back at the house with bindings and duct tape or even drugs. She was a light burden. He would have walked at an easy pace, unafraid of detection. The woods would have been dark enough to give him plenty of cover.

The vision was so vivid that Jake felt compelled to step off the path and allow the imagined kidnapper to pass. Then he moved quickly along the trail until the landscape began to shift from deep forest into a craggy hillock. He'd walked a good two miles from Reggie's house and now found himself in the middle of nowhere. No sign of life except for a distant tumbledown farmhouse that had been eaten by kudzu.

He followed a ten-foot metal fence until he came to a padlocked gate. Posted signs discouraged exploration of the cave without an experienced guide and waivers from the property owner. However, as Lyle Crowder had mentioned the day before, there was nothing preventing anyone from climbing over the fence and descending at their own risk.

Jake tested the metal links for an electrical current before he climbed over. Landing softly on the other side, he took a moment to scout his surroundings before scrambling up the rugged terrain to the cave entrance— a narrow hole between two boulders that dropped straight down into the earth. Crouching at the edge, he angled his flashlight beam inside the natural cylinder. About fifteen to twenty feet down, the passageway appeared to open up into a larger cavern.

He lowered himself to the ground and hung over the opening, shining the flashlight beam along the limestone walls as far down as he could see. Time and erosion had carved plenty of hand- and footholds in the soft rock. Descent would be easy. No need for a rope and harness.

Even so, he still had no intention of going down into the cave alone. Hadn't he cautioned both Thea and Lyle Crowder against that very thing? Besides, it seemed like a waste of time. People far more familiar with the underground structure than he was had already searched the passageways.

So why did he linger? Why did he suddenly hear Thea's voice reminding him that he'd found the twig figures in the woods *after* the police and volunteers had conducted a thorough canvass?

No sooner had the image of those strange totems materialized in his head than a sound came to him straight up out of the earth. He could have sworn he heard the odd clacking of the twig bodies as they bumped together in the breeze. He listened intently, trying to determine if the noise might have come from the woods rather than from deep inside the cave. The hollow melody drifted up to him again, followed by a different sound—a faint, unidentifiable mewling.

A chill skated down Jake's backbone. He let himself imagine for a moment the end of the kidnapper's journey. He would have come out of the woods near the fence just as Jake had. Scaling the chain links with his precious burden would have been a challenge unless he was exceptionally strong or had cut the fence earlier. Jake hadn't seen any holes, but the damage could have been hidden by scrub brush. Then what? Had he climbed into the cave with Kylie and hidden her body in a tunnel or simply tossed her over the edge? Left for dead in a pitch-black environment, could the child have crawled deep inside one of the dry passageways to hide? Was that how the search party had missed her?

More than likely the kidnapper hadn't come this way at all. Maybe the sound Jake heard was nothing more than a draft of air whistling through one of the tunnels.

But what if it wasn't? What if Kylie was down there somewhere? Still alive and whimpering in pain and fear as she ran out of time and air? What if she crawled into one of the passageways filled with water? Jake knew he would never have a moment's peace until he made certain.

He called his second-in-command and told him where he was and what he intended to do. The agent responded in alarm. "Sounds like a risky move, boss. Shouldn't you wait for backup? Be even better if we can find a local guide to go down with us."

"We may not have that kind of time," Jake said. "I saw a diagram of the cave in Chief Bowden's office. I can pull up a similar image on my phone before I go in. As long as I stick to the main passageways, I should be fine. Gear up and get here as soon as you can."

Jake thought about calling Thea, but she'd come running and he didn't want to take the chance she'd crawl down into the pit to look for him. He wasn't the overly protective type when it came to a trained agent, but Thea had admitted earlier that she wasn't physically or mentally herself since the accident. Under the best of circumstances, a cave environment could be disorienting. It was too easy to wander along a passageway and become lost and confused by the strange topography. He'd let her know his position as soon as his backup arrived.

Tucking away the flashlight, he bent and scooped up some loose pebbles from the dirt to make a little pile beside the entrance. Then he squeezed through the crevice and lowered himself inside.

So this is the Devil's Pit, he thought as he felt for handholds and footings in the limestone. He enjoyed wall climbing at his gym, so the relatively short descent wasn't much of a challenge, nor did he expect to have any trouble getting out. The biggest obstacles were the narrowness of the opening and the absence of light once he'd descended a few feet. The close confines made him a little uneasy at first, but then he was through the narrow shaft in a matter of seconds and, after maneuvering over the rocky debris at the bottom, he could stand upright. He took out the flashlight and swept the beam over the cavern.

He'd done some cave diving in his college days,

strictly amateur and always with an experienced guide. Dry caves were a whole different ecosystem. He turned off the flashlight and stood in the dark for several minutes, letting his eyes adjust as he tried to tune into the keening he'd heard from above. When nothing came to him, he wondered again if he'd let his imagination get the better of him. What if he hadn't? What if Kylie was down there somewhere?

"Kylie! Kylie Buchanan! If you can hear my voice, call out to me, okay? Don't be afraid. I'm here to take you home."

His voice echoed back to him. Jake waited until the resonance died away before he called to her again. "Kylie, can you hear me?"

Nothing.

After his eyes and equilibrium had adjusted to the blackness, he turned on the flashlight and shone it once again around the large cavern. A narrow opening in the wall opposite the entrance presumably led back into a second cavern. From what he remembered of the diagram, this particular cave system was a string-of-pearls formation—a series of tight tunnels opening into larger caverns one after the other for a couple of miles or so with dozens of belly-crawl passageways that led to nowhere. A headlamp would have made exploring those dead-end spaces easier, but he'd have to make do with his flashlight. At least it was waterproof if he ran into submerged areas in the passageways.

As he had aboveground, he marked the shaft where he'd climbed down with a pile of pebbles before he set out. He judged the temperature to be a mild seventy degrees or so, a welcome respite from the relentless heat on the surface. Crossing the floor, he aimed his light down the first passageway. Someone had left a candle and matches at the entrance, but he didn't use them. He left another pile of stones beside the candle and entered the first tunnel. Crawling over the loose rocks in the narrow space would have been tricky but not impossible for a four-year-old child. The image drove Jake forward.

He emerged from the passageway into another room. He could hear water dripping nearby, and the air became dank and musty. The speleothems were more pronounced in this cavern. The eerie limestone formations glistened in the beam of his light. Curious, he took out his phone. No signal.

According to the diagram, an underground river ran beneath the cave floor. From here on in, he might well come upon passageways at least partially filled with water. The prospect was unnerving, but he wasn't about to turn back. He left his stone bread crumbs at the entrance and moved into the next passage. Several feet in, he had to drop to his hands and knees and then to his elbows and belly. The stone was wet and muddy beneath him, but at least he found no standing water.

The third and largest cavern yet was riddled with tunnels. Jake wanted to believe the search party had been through every square inch of those channels, but the territory was rugged with lots of dead ends and, in those first critical hours, even professionals could get careless in the initial frenzy.

He felt the onset of a very bad feeling. There were too many places to hide a small body down here. Too many narrow tunnels and tubes a child might have squeezed into and become lost and disoriented.

"Hello?" His voice echoed back to him, as hollow as the clacking figures. "Kylie, can you hear me?"

He waited for the sound of his voice to die away again before he called out, "Don't be afraid. I'm a police officer. I'm here to take you to your mommy."

He could have sworn he heard a shuffling sound from one of the tunnels. Squatting in front of the entrance, he shone the light into the narrow channel. "Kylie?"

Something flew out at him. The sudden movement startled him and he lost his balance, sprawling backward on the floor as he threw up an arm to cover his head. The light had disturbed a colony of bats. Jake waited for the migration to pass and then, gagging at the smell, crawled far enough into the tunnel to see all the way to the dead end. Nothing.

Either he'd imagined the shuffling sound or he'd heard the bats stirring. Being belowground could play tricks on the senses. Not to mention the havoc certain fungi and bacteria could wreak on one's perception. He paused to clear his head. Was he crazy for coming down here alone? Yes, but he'd had no choice. Nor was backtracking to the entrance and crawling up out of the pit to wait for reinforcements an option. That would take too much time when he was very much afraid every second counted. His team knew where he was and he'd left a trail. Nothing for him to do now but keep going.

Methodically, he made his way around the third cavern, checking the dead-end tunnels that he could fit into and angling his light into the others. When he finished, he stacked stones in front of the next passageway before he entered.

He exited into another chamber where the underground river bubbled up into a large pool surrounded by slick limestone walls. He didn't immediately see another tunnel although, according to the diagram, the cave went on for at least another mile or so. Maybe the passageway into the next opening was underwater. Given the challenging terrain, he didn't see how Kylie could have made it this far by herself.

Crouching on a slippery ledge above the pool, he shone the flashlight beam over the water where something bobbled on the surface.

THEA USED THE spare key hidden in the flowerpot to unlock the front door. It had been years since she'd been inside her mother's house. She stepped across the threshold and paused to take stock of the changes. The couch and paint color were different. The armchair in front of the TV had been slipcovered, but she recognized the bulky shape. Everything else was the same, careworn but clean and tidy, with very little clutter except for a stack of home improvement magazines on the coffee table.

Her mother had only been away for two nights, but the air seemed stale, as if the place had been closed up for a very long time. Thea wrinkled her nose at the fusty odor as a shiver skimmed across her nerve endings. Something was wrong in here. She couldn't put her finger on it. Told herself it was probably nothing more than her imagination. Yet she could almost feel the air settle around her as if someone had moved out of the room just ahead of her.

Unsnapping her cross-body bag, she slipped her hand inside and gripped her weapon. "Hello? Anybody here?"

It occurred to her that Taryn Buchanan might have come by to pick up something she'd left behind or even to spend time in the room where her little girl had been taken. Thea didn't draw her weapon. Instead, she left the bag unsnapped and resting against her hip as she moved across the room.

Unease trailed her down the hallway, past Reggie's bedroom and the hall bathroom to the second door on the right. Thea's hand hovered over the knob before she pushed the door open and entered. She'd grown up in this bedroom. Had spent her childhood, adolescence and teenage years alone inside these four walls after Maya had been taken. But when she looked back, everything that came after her sister's disappearance seemed hazy and surreal, as if she'd sleepwalked through her life until she'd been old enough to move out of this room, out of this house. Even then, the past had followed her. She'd just become more adept at eluding the ghosts.

The musty odor was more prevalent inside this room and the temperature was uncomfortably warm. Thea wondered if Reggie had adjusted the thermostat or turned off the AC altogether before she'd left the house. That would be like her. Frugal out of necessity and habit.

One of the twin beds had been removed a long time ago. The other had been pushed up against the wall facing the window. After her sister had first gone missing,

Reggie had moved Thea into her bedroom and she'd slept in here on Maya's bed. But Thea hadn't been able to stay away. She'd get up in the middle of the night and return to her own bed, where she would lie awake for hours staring into the darkness, waiting for Maya to come home. Finally, Reggie had moved back to her room, but she would leave both doors open to the hallway all night. Sometimes Thea would hear her pacing through the house. Sometimes Reggie would come into the room and check the lock on the window. Thea always pretended to sleep. To this day, she didn't know why. Or maybe she did. Maybe she just didn't want to think too hard about her reason.

Shaking off the memories, she walked around the room. A few remnants of her teenage years remained, along with evidence of Kylie Buchanan's brief stay. A coloring book on the desk and a small suitcase in the closet. Some neatly folded clothes on the dresser. Not much here to entertain a four-year-old child.

Maybe Taryn had already moved the rest of their things into the apartment, or maybe she'd been in such a hurry to leave Russ Buchanan's house that she'd fled to Reggie's with only the basic necessities. Thea thought about her conversation with Jake regarding Taryn's possible role in her daughter's kidnapping. Had she set up the abduction to get the child away from an abusive father?

Having met Buchanan face-to-face, Thea could well imagine Taryn's desperation. A man like that would stop at little to keep his family under his thumb. But would he go so far as to kidnap his own daughter as punishment for his wife's betrayal?

On and on her thoughts raced as she walked over to the window and glanced out. In broad daylight with the sun shining down on all the flowerbeds, the backyard looked lovely and peaceful. By nightfall, however, the atmosphere changed. The woods were very dark even under a full moon. Thea used to see all manner of shadows at the edge of those trees. She would stare into the night certain someone lurked behind the fence, waiting until Reggie's bedroom light went out before creeping across the yard to Thea's window.

For years, nightmares had tormented her sleep until she'd eventually outgrown her fear of the woods. They still came back now and then when she was tired or sick or had suffered an emotional trauma. She still occasionally dreamed about those whispering shadows standing over her bed.

Was someone out there now? Thea knew she was letting the past and her imagination prod her uneasiness, but she could have sworn she saw someone at the corner of the latticework potting shed. Maybe Jake was searching the outbuildings before he set out for the woods. She opened the window and leaned out. "Jake?"

No answer. No sound of any kind except for a faint *click-click-click* as the windmill rotated in the breeze.

Returning to the hallway, she backtracked to Reggie's door. Her bedroom was smaller than Thea's. Funny, she'd never noticed that before. The windows looked out on the side yard and street. If anyone pulled up in the driveway in the middle of the night, the head-lights would arc across the ceiling and wake Reggie.

The furnishings were spare and simple: bed, night-stand and dresser, a matching set. Nothing fancy or frilly, but serviceable and every piece paid for, no doubt. That had always been important to Reggie, and a good lesson for her daughter. Thea owed nothing to anyone.

She went over to the closet and riffled through her mother's belongings until she located the box she was looking for pushed back in a corner. She doubted she would find the other half of the torn photograph among Reggie's keepsakes, but it was worth taking a look.

The task of going through her mother's old picture box was both painful and tedious. Thea was struck anew at the scarcity of individual photographs of her and Maya. They were always together. Smiling. Hold-ing hands. *Two peas in a pod.* After the abduction, there were hardly any snapshots of Thea at all. It was as if their whole world had stopped on that night. Sometimes it had seemed to Thea as if Reggie could barely stand to look at her after Maya went missing.

She'd gone through about half of the photographs when her head jerked up and she listened intently to the quiet house. The sound of ruffling paper came to her from the hallway. She'd left the window open to air out the other room. Maybe a breeze had caught the pages of Kylie's coloring book.

Thea rose and slipped across the room to the hall-way door. The ruffling came from her right, toward the front of the house. She followed the sound back down the hallway and into the kitchen. The house had grown so warm that the air conditioner had finally kicked on. A draft from one of the vents had caught the edge of a child's drawing pinned to the refrigerator. Kylie's artwork, Thea thought with a pang. But then she saw the painstakingly scrawled names above the crudely drawn figures and her heart thudded. *Me. Sissy.*

Not Kylie's artwork. Maya's.

Two stick figures with red hearts colored onto their torsos and yellow hair sprouting from their circular heads.

The drawing was so reminiscent of the totems Jake had found in the woods that Thea didn't see how it could be a coincidence. Why had she not seen it before? Someone had deliberately turned Maya's innocent rendering of her and her beloved Sissy into something dark and grotesque. It was as if Maya's abductor had come back after all these years to taunt her family, using little Kylie Buchanan as a pawn in some sick, perverted game.

Derrick Sway would have known about that drawing. Reggie had always displayed their artwork on the refrigerator. He would have seen it every time he'd made a trip into the kitchen for a beer. Had he kept that drawing with him in prison, along with the torn photograph of Maya? Had he returned it to Reggie's refrigerator after he'd taken Kylie Buchanan?

Thea removed the magnet and clutched her sister's artwork as she sat down heavily at the kitchen table. The drawing hadn't been there all along. The police would surely have taken note of it during a search of the house. Someone had come into Reggie's home after the kidnapping and pinned the artwork to the refrigerator, where Thea was certain to find it.

She and Jake had been so wrong about motive. The twig totems were never meant to connect Kylie Buchanan's abduction to Maya's. The nearly identical carvings with their hideous grinning faces and hollowed-out eyes had been left in the woods behind Reggie's house as an offering—or a warning—to Maya's twin.

THE DOLL BOBBLED gently on the surface of the black water, seemingly caught in two opposing currents that propelled her in a gentle circle around the pool. When she floated into Jake's light, the glass eyes glinted eerily so that, for a moment, he had the wildest notion she was alive.

It's a doll, not a child.

Left deep inside a cave.

Hunkering on the rocky ledge above the pool, he grabbed for an outstretched arm, but the currents carried her out of his reach. He trailed his light after her, recognizing the golden hair and pink dress from the description Taryn Buchanan had provided to the police. She'd claimed the only thing missing from Kylie's room after the abduction was the child's favorite doll. Jake thought about another doll that had been dug up in a wooden box containing Maya Lamb's DNA. Two abandoned dolls found in underground places. Two children taken through the same bedroom window twenty-eight years apart. More and more it seemed as if the same predator had taken both girls. Or else someone was working very hard to make him think so.

The doll seemed a good indication that Kylie had been in the cave at some point, but where was she now? Jake shone the light into the pool, dreading what he might see beyond his reflection. Divers would have to go down there. He felt an urgency to search the water himself, but without the right equipment, the effort would be dangerous and futile.

As he watched, the doll began to circle faster in tighter loops toward the center of the pool. An eddy or whirlpool sucked her under, but she surfaced a few moments later, still floating just beyond Jake's reach. He flattened himself on the wet ledge and cupped his hand through the cold water, trying to pull the doll toward him. Released from the eddy, she floated lazily around the pool, the circles widening until she bumped up against the rock wall.

So intent was Jake on his task that he hadn't a clue someone had entered the cavern behind him until a shadow wavered briefly on the glinting water. Lying facedown on the slippery ledge—one hand clutching the flashlight, the other submerged in the pool—he found himself caught unaware in a vulnerable position. So much for his uncanny instincts. The irony of his predicament registered a split second before the back of his skull exploded in pain. Dazed, he rolled and reached for his weapon as he put up a hand to deflect the second blow. A hard kick in his side and the next thing he knew, he was underwater.

Something grazed his cheek. The doll or something living? Trying to fight off the shock of pain and icy water, he relaxed his muscles so that his body could float upward. Too late, he realized he was caught in the whirlpool that had sucked the doll under moments earlier. His weight had carried him deeper. Several feet below the surface, the undercurrents were much stronger. Jake had heard of sinkholes at the bottom of rivers that created maelstroms so powerful even expert swimmers could become trapped and pulled to their death.

Confronted with an unknown force dragging him down, possibly into an abyss, he did what most people would do in his place—he panicked and lashed out with his arms and legs. He knew the frenzied effort would quickly expend his energy, eventually forcing him to inhale water and drown. He *knew* this. Yet for a few precious seconds, he fought frantically against the swirling waters until his brain finally processed the situation in a rational manner. *Stay calm and hold your breath.*

Eventually the currents would change their flow and direction and he would pop back to the surface the way the doll had done earlier. *Just ride it out.* But the whirlpool spun him around in ever-tightening circles and he soon grew dizzy and terrifyingly disoriented. It was one thing to tell himself to remain calm, doing so while completely blinded underwater was something else altogether. Time and again, he had to fight the urge to try to break free. *Expend energy. Inhale water. Drown.*

The circles finally began to widen and slow. Jake's instinct was to swim sideways out of the weakened current. Far below him, however, his flashlight was still caught in the dying eddy, creating an eerie illumination as the waterproof housing spun in the water. Common sense told him to let it go. He couldn't take the chance on getting caught in an even stronger whirlpool if he went deeper, one that could either bash him into the rock wall or suck him into an underwater crater where he would be hopelessly lost with or without the flashlight.

He supposed it was human nature to gravitate toward light. Still dizzy and disoriented, he found himself following that swirling illumination until his lungs screamed for relief and he realized he was fighting an unwinnable battle. He couldn't reach the flashlight. It was sinking too fast and he was quickly running out of air and energy. Abandoning the light, he changed course and swam in the opposite direction.

What if the light wasn't sinking? What if the buoyancy of the rubber housing carried the light upward and, rather than swimming toward the surface, Jake was going deeper into the vortex?

For a heart-stopping moment, he had no idea which way was up or down. Without light from the surface, he had nothing to guide him, not even the bubbles from his expelled air. He tried once again to relax his body so that he could rise to the surface, but maybe he was descending instead.

This is why you don't go into a cave alone.

Okay, think. The flashlight was waterproof and designed to float. Logic told him that once free of the undercurrents, the unit would rise to the surface. *Follow the light.*

Decision made, he reversed course yet again and swam toward the radiance. He couldn't have been under water for much more than a minute, and yet it seemed he'd been down forever. When his head finally broke the surface, he gulped air on a gasp and swam in total darkness until his body scraped up against the rock wall. He found a slippery handhold and clung for dear life as he waited for the residual dizziness to pass.

He looked around for the flashlight. The bulb must have gone out or maybe the light had floated into an underwater passageway. His phone was gone, too, but at least he still had his weapon. Gripping the slick wall, he tuned into the silence. His assailant could be anywhere in the pitch-blackness.

After a few moments, he could feel the undercurrents tugging him away from the wall. The force came in concentric waves, each stronger than the last. He searched for more handholds in the rock. Using the last of his energy, he hoisted himself out of the water and onto the ledge, uncertain that he was even in the same cavern. Maybe the currents had carried him beneath the wall into another chamber. Without a flashlight or phone, he would be hard-pressed to find his way out.

Don't panic.

That was quickly becoming his mantra, he realized. Help was on the way. His team knew he was down here. They'd search every nook and cranny until they found him. But what if they couldn't find him?

Don't panic.

He felt along the ledge to determine the width. Enough room to navigate if he was careful. He rose slowly, hands above his head to make sure he could stand upright. Then he shuffled away from the edge of the pool until his shoulder grazed the limestone wall. Earlier, he'd piled pebbles in front of the passageway from which he'd emerged into the cavern. All he had to do was make his way around the wall until he found the stones. *If* they were still there and *if* he was in the same cavern. He wouldn't let himself dwell on either possibility.

He crept forward on the ledge until he felt a draft on his wet skin. If he hadn't been soaked to the bone, he might never have noticed that whisper of fresh air. Now he turned slowly until the breeze skimmed his wet face. He walked toward the waft, guided by little more than instinct, determination and a faint melodic clacking that chilled him more deeply than the bottomless pool.

Chapter Eight

Thea stepped through the gate behind Reggie's house and paused to scan the tree line. Jake had been gone for an awfully long time. She wasn't so much alarmed as she was impatient. He was a trained federal agent with keen instincts. He could more than hold his own in almost any situation. But Maya's drawing was a significant discovery and Thea was anxious to discuss the implications. At least, that's what she told herself.

She flicked an uneasy glance over her shoulder, unable to shake the niggling worry that someone had been in the house just ahead of her. Her sister's artwork hadn't appeared out of thin air. Someone had deliberately left it on the refrigerator for her or Reggie to find. But why? If Derrick Sway had taken Kylie Buchanan out of mistaken identity or retribution, why would he come back here in broad daylight? Was he that confident he could elude detection, or did a craving that superseded caution drive him? The same dark need that compelled murderers to return to the scene of the crime and kidnappers to join in the search for their victims.

Turning back to the woods, Thea started to call out

Jake's name, but the utter silence of her surroundings
stilled her. Earlier she could have sworn she'd spotted
someone at the corner of the potting shed, but she'd
chalked the sighting up to imagination or shadows.
Now she whirled again, this time searching all across
her mother's backyard and probing the hiding places
between the outbuildings. Then tilting her head, she
skimmed the treetops. The mild breeze drifting through
the leaves seemed to whisper of danger. Of something
so dark and insidious that it shouldn't be spoken aloud.

Fishing her phone from her bag, she called Jake's
cell, left a voice mail and then sent a brief text.

Where are you?

No response. She waited a moment and sent another.

Jake? You okay? Text me back.

Maybe the trees were blocking the signal, she decided, but apprehension slid like an icy finger down
her backbone. She returned the phone to her bag and
removed her weapon, slipping it into the back of her
jeans for easier access. She wished she'd worn her hol-
ster, but nothing she could do about that now.

Taking another scan of the trees, she set out. Mos-
quitos buzzed around her ears as sweat trickled down
her back. It was barely ten o'clock and the heat and
humidity had already become stifling. A few hundred
yards in, she stopped once more to listen for signs of
life. Jake had to be nearby. He was on foot. How far

could he go? But if he was that close, he was surely receiving her texts. Why wasn't he answering her? It wasn't like him to simply vanish when he knew she'd be concerned.

The sound of rustling leaves came from somewhere behind her and she spun, her senses on high alert. "Jake?"

No answer, but now she heard the crackle of trodden underbrush as someone advanced quickly down the path in her direction, still concealed by the thick vegetation. Not Jake. He would have responded. This was someone who seemed intent on overtaking her.

A bird took flight from a treetop, startling her. Drawing her weapon, she automatically flexed her knees and extended both arms straight out as she brought the sight to her eyes. She waited for the space of a heartbeat, her attention 100 percent focused before she called out, "Federal agent! Come out now with your hands where I can see them!"

For a man of his age and size, Derrick Sway's furtive movements struck Thea as almost uncanny. One moment the trail was clear, and then in the next instant, he plunged through the low-hanging branches and halted in front of her, a hulking, formidable presence. He'd been so much on her mind since Jake had showed her the torn photograph that, for a crazy moment, Thea thought she might have conjured him from thin air. But no, he was there and all too real. Either he'd followed her from Reggie's house or he'd already been in the woods, heard her on the trail and circled through the trees to come up behind her.

In the ensuing silence of their face-off, Thea took in several details about his appearance and committed them to memory in case she would later need to give a description. Ragged jeans. Sleeveless black T-shirt. Steel-toed work boots even in the scorching heat. Scar across his right cheek. Hair closely cropped, allowing the ink on his scalp to show through.

What struck her the most forcefully about his appearance was how much he'd changed since she'd last seen him. He hadn't just aged. The years of his incarceration had transformed him from brooding hoodlum to sneering psychopath. If Thea remembered correctly, he was only a couple of years older than Reggie, probably just over fifty with the brawny physique of a middle-aged man who lifted weights not for health or conceit, but for the ability to inflict pain on anyone who crossed him.

He had a pistol stuffed in the waistband of his jeans. That he hadn't already drawn on her was a testament to his supreme confidence in his physical abilities. He was ready for her, though. His hands were splayed out from his sides as if he were waiting for her to make the first move.

"Stay where you are," she warned.

His eyes narrowed to slits as he grinned. "You pull that trigger, little girl, you better make damn certain it's a kill shot."

"Not a problem," she said with steely determination. "Remove your weapon and toss it toward me. Do it now!"

He hesitated a fraction of a second before removing the pistol and dropping it to the ground.

"Kick it over here," Thea said. "Then down on your knees, hands behind your head." The adrenaline was pumping so hard through her veins she sucked in air, trying to control her racing heartbeat. She couldn't let him see how badly he'd caught her off guard. She couldn't let him know that the very sight of him had churned her stomach and beaded cold sweat upon her brow.

As the reality of the situation crashed down on her—alone in the woods with the man who may very well have killed her twin sister—Thea wanted nothing so much as to bring her weapon to his temple to force him to tell her why a picture of Maya had been found in his possession twenty-eight years after she'd gone missing. She wanted to slam her fist into his vile, grinning face and make him own up to what he'd done to a four-year-old child.

She could do none of that, of course. Professional conduct aside, he would physically overpower her if he got half a chance. Her only recourse was to hold him there until backup arrived. But she didn't take out her phone to call for help. Not yet. Instead, she eyed him coldly as she fought her baser instincts.

He lowered himself to his knees and laced his fingers behind his head, all the while returning her scrutiny with that blood-chilling grin. What was he up to? Why had he given up his weapon so easily?

Thea kicked the pistol aside, keeping a bead and her distance. "What are you doing out here?"

"Just out for a morning stroll." Mockery dripped around the edges of his voice. "I always did like walking in the woods. Lots of secrets buried beneath some of these trees."

Like her sister's remains?

He tilted his head and closed his eyes as if drawing in a scent only he could detect.

"What secrets?" Thea demanded.

"They wouldn't be secret if I told you, now would they?" He wasn't afraid of being arrested. He certainly wasn't afraid of her. Thea reminded herself she had to be careful he didn't bait her into doing something foolish. "I'm not breaking any laws, so what's your beef with me, officer?"

"Agent. Possession of a firearm by a felon is a felony," she said. "That alone will get you one to three."

"How do you know I'm a felon?"

"All that prison ink is a pretty good indication."

He cocked his head. "Nah, I don't think that's it. You remember me, don't you, Sissy?"

White-hot anger wrenched at her resolve as sweat trickled down the side of her face. She resisted the urge to wipe it away with her shoulder. "Don't call me that."

He knew he'd hit a nerve. She was making this too easy for him. His grin slid into a leer. "Yeah, you remember me, all right. I'm a hard man to forget. Just ask your mama." He ran his tongue slowly over his lips. "That gal was a real wildcat back before she got religion."

The thought of their intimacy physically sickened Thea. She swallowed back her nausea as she filed away more details. Mud on his jeans and the bottoms of his work boots. Fresh scratches on his hands and arms.

Some of his tattoos were more than a little disturbing. In addition to the usual prison black and white—dots on his knuckles, spider web at his elbow—he had what appeared to be occult symbolism on his biceps and along the side of his neck disappearing down into his shirt. The imagery reminded Thea of the mysterious twin totems Jake had found in these woods near this very spot. She'd sensed from the first there was something sinister about those depictions. Something meant to instill fear.

"I'll ask you again," she said. "What are you doing out here?"

"And I'll give you the same answer. I'm out for a morning stroll."

She gave him a hard, knowing glare. "You know what I think? I think you came back looking for something you left behind."

His eyes glinted with amusement but something dark and depraved lurked beneath the surface. "Just a simple walk, nothing more."

"With every law enforcement agency in the state looking for you? I don't think so."

"Let them look," he said with an unconcerned shrug. "If you had anything on me, you'd have these woods swarming with cops. Instead, there's no one around for miles but you and me. Know what *I* think? You don't want anyone else joining our little party just yet. You want me all to yourself. You know if you take me in, I'll demand a lawyer. As long as it's just the two of us out here in the middle of nowhere, you might get me to talking. Maybe I'll let something slip." He gave her a nod of admiration. "You like to live dangerously, don't you, girl? I like that."

"Then you'll talk to me?"

"I might if you ask the right questions."

"Why did you have a torn photograph of my sister in your possession?"

He scowled at her. "What photograph?"

Thea wasn't in the mood. "Don't play games. You know damn well the photo I mean. The one found hidden behind the baseboard in a bedroom closet at your mother's house."

He lifted a brow as something indefinable flickered in his eyes. "Ever think someone else might have put it there?"

"No."

"Because a cop has never been known to plant evidence, right?"

"Just answer the question," Thea demanded. "Where did you get that photograph?" *And why did you cut me out of the image and singe the edge?*

"Don't know about any photograph. Final answer."

Thea let his vague response stand for a moment. "Then let's go back to my original question. Why are you lurking around in the woods behind my mother's house?"

"The truth? I saw you from a distance and thought you were Reggie. Honest mistake. It's been a while since I saw her up close and you favor her enough to fool me." His gaze dropped. "It's the way you wear those jeans, I expect."

Thea suppressed a shudder. "Were you in her house just now?"

"Why would I be in her house?"

"That's not an answer."

"Can't make things too easy for you unless I get a little something in return."

Thea's voice hardened as she battled her temper. "This isn't a negotiation."

"Everything's a negotiation. It's just that this time I'm the one in the catbird seat."

"Funny, because last time I checked, I'm the one with the gun," Thea said.

"For now." He dipped his head and looked up at her in a way that sent a shiver straight through her heart.

She subtly adjusted her stance. "You say you mistook me for my mother. Why would you follow her into the woods?"

"That's an easy one. Reggie and me got an old score to settle."

"What score?"

"That's between her and me."

"You've been out of prison for months. Why come here now?" Thea pressed.

"After ten years in that hellhole, I had a lot of scores to settle. Saved the best for last." He shook his head slightly as he looked her up and down once more. "So Reggie Lamb done raised herself a cop. Who would have ever thought?"

"Why does that surprise you?"

"Your mama wasn't exactly the law-and-order type when I knew her. She was up for anything back in the day. Always dragging you damn kids with us all over creation." He squinted up at her. "You remember sleeping in the back seat of my car?"

"No."

"That's probably a good thing for your sake. Might have seen something that was bad for your health."

"Like what?"

He gave her a meaningful look, but didn't answer. "I used to wonder what you girls would look like when you grew up. Reggie was a mighty fine piece of—"

"Watch your mouth," Thea snapped.

He pursed his lips in appreciation. "You're not so hard on the eyes, either, but the other one? Maya? I could tell even then she'd be a real little heartbreaker someday."

Bile rose in Thea's throat. She could feel her hands start to tremble in rage. *Don't take the bait. Don't let him goad you into letting down your guard.* She pulled in air. "Did you take her?"

"Which one?" His drawl still had that mocking edge.

As much as Thea wanted to learn the truth about her sister—and she intended to do exactly that—there was a more pressing issue at hand. "What do you know about Kylie Buchanan's disappearance?"

"Only that she's long gone by now."

"How do you know that?"

"Use your head, girl. It's been…what? Two days since she went missing? Reason should tell you she's already dead or on way out of the country. Either way, you're wasting your time searching these woods."

"There's only one way you can be that certain," Thea said.

"Nah, I'm just being realistic."

She lowered her voice as she tried to filter out her anger and disgust. *Just keep him talking, see what you can learn.* "Like you said, there's no one around but you and me. You'll notice I haven't arrested or read you your rights. That means anything you say can't be used against you in a criminal case. Tell me the truth. Do you know where she is?"

His expression turned sly. "Which one?"

He was enjoying this too much. He knew he was getting under her skin. "Are you admitting you took my sister?"

"If I say yes, will you let me go?"

She tightened her grip on the firearm. "Confess and find out."

His laugh was a low, ugly rumble. "I'm not confessing to anything, but even if I did, you couldn't lay a hand on me. I could get up and walk away this very instant and you wouldn't dare shoot me. Know why? Because if you really believe I nabbed that little girl, you won't risk killing the one person you think can tell you where she is."

"Try me," Thea dared him. "I'm an excellent shot. I can make you wish you were dead without hitting anything vital."

"Go ahead," he said as he rose slowly to his feet. "Let's see how good you really are."

Thea shot off a round close enough to stop him dead in his tracks. Tree bark exploded near his head. He picked a splinter from his cheek as he sized her up. No longer taunting or leering, he had the look of a man who would enjoy ripping her heart out with his teeth.

He spread his hands at his sides.

"Don't do anything stupid," Thea said. "I don't want to shoot you, but I will if I have to."

He was right, though. How could she risk putting him down when he might be the only link to Kylie's whereabouts? But if she didn't do something quick, the confrontation could rapidly escalate into a kill-or-be-killed situation. She mentally ran through her options, which were few from where she stood.

Then something unexpected happened. A male shout came from somewhere nearby. She thought, at first, it must be Jake. When he called out a second time, she realized she'd never heard the voice before.

"Did you hear what I said?" he bellowed. "We're out here looking for the missing child. Stop shooting before you hit someone!"

Thea responded to the faceless stranger without taking her eyes off Sway. "I'm Agent Thea Lamb with the FBI. Stay where you are and identify yourself."

Silence. Then, "You're Reggie Lamb's daughter?" The underbrush rustled close by. A man rushed out of the trees.

"I said stay where you are!" Thea yelled.

Instead of using the distraction to his advantage, Sway pivoted toward the stranger. Thea kept her gaze and weapon trained on Sway as she observed the new-comer from her periphery. He'd stopped short a few feet from the path to take stock of the situation. From what she could see, he was of medium height and build with longish brown hair and wire-rimmed glasses. He wore jeans, sneakers and a white T-shirt with some kind of logo on the pocket. Nothing stood out about him except that he seemed to know her mother.

"What's going on here?" he asked, his gaze moving from Sway to Thea and back to Sway.

"Stay back, sir," Thea cautioned. "I'm taking this man into custody."

The stranger adjusted his glasses as he took an awkward step back from the path. "What's he done?"

"Go on about your business and let me handle this," Thea said.

The stranger halted his retreat as his gaze shot again to Derrick Sway. "Wait a minute. I know who you are. I saw your picture at the command center this morning. You're the ex-con everyone's looking for." He swung back around to Thea. "I'm Eldon Mossey. Your mother is a good friend of mine."

He certainly didn't match the image of the charismatic country preacher Thea had visualized in her head. His appearance was the very definition of nondescript. And yet even as her first instinct was to dismiss him as a harmless bystander, she caught a look in Derrick Sway's eyes that made her wonder again why he hadn't attacked when he'd had the opportunity. What was going on here? Did the two of them know each other? Had she interrupted a clandestine meeting in the woods?

As if sensing her suspicions, Eldon said quickly, "Kylie's mother and I came out here to look for her. We couldn't sit around in the police station all day and do nothing. We split up to cover more ground. When I heard the gunshot, I was worried an inexperienced deputy or civilian volunteer might have gotten trigger happy."

A young woman came hurrying out of the woods and halted behind him. She was a few years younger than Mossey—probably in her midtwenties, though her snarled ponytail and gaunt frame made her look much younger on first glance. Her pale blond hair shimmered golden in the spangled light. For some reason, Thea thought of the yellow hair that sprouted from the figures in Maya's drawing and from the wood totems.

Even with her drawn features and the dark circles beneath her eyes, Taryn Buchanan was a very beautiful young woman. Beautiful, fragile and tragic. Catnip to a man like Russ Buchanan and possibly to Eldon Mossey.

Taryn came up beside Eldon, breathless from her sprint through the trees. "I heard a gunshot—" She broke off on a gasp when she saw Derrick Sway, who had hardly moved a muscle. Thea had no doubt he was planning something. He wouldn't wait around passively for her backup to arrive, let alone for her to put him in cuffs. He was biding his time for the right opportunity.

Mossey put out a hand as if to hold Taryn back. "Stay behind me. This is Reggie's daughter. She's taking this man into custody."

"What's going on?" Taryn asked in a shocked voice. "Who is he?"

"We saw his photograph earlier at the command center, remember? His name is Derrick Sway."

Taryn let out a gasp as her hand flew to her throat.

Mossey tried to put a protective arm around her shoulders, but she stumbled out of his reach. Her eyes widened as she stared at Sway. Thea saw something in the blue depths that alarmed her.

"Stay calm," she advised, but she feared she was quickly losing control of the situation.

Taryn's keening rose to a shrill howl. "You're a monster! You took my baby! Where is she? What have you done to her? *Tell me where she is!*"

Mossey started toward her. "Taryn, honey—"

"Don't touch me!" She seemed on the verge of hyperventilating as her fingers clenched into tight fists at her sides.

Sway pounced on her vulnerability. "What say you and me take a stroll through the woods? You treat me right and maybe I'll tell you what you want to know," he taunted.

Before Mossey could stop her, Taryn lunged for Sway, playing right into his hands. In the blink of an eye, he had her by the throat, pulling her back against him as he whipped out a knife.

"Put down your piece or I'll slit her throat and gut her like a pig," he warned.

Thea had no doubt he would do exactly that and laugh while doing so. She bent and placed her firearm on the ground.

Taryn had been struggling to free herself from his grip, but now she went limp as her eyes darkened with fear.

"Don't hurt her," Mossey pleaded. "Just let her go and walk away."

"Throw your phones over here," Sway commanded. When they complied, he smashed them with the heel of his boot. "Here's what's about to happen. She's coming with me. If either of you tries to follow, she dies. If I see or hear sirens, she dies." He started backing toward the trees, his arm still around Taryn's throat. When she stumbled, he lifted her off the ground, crushing her windpipe. She clawed at his beefy arm, gasping frantically for air. He eased the pressure but didn't let her go. Within seconds, the trees swallowed them up.

Thea retrieved her gun and started after them. Eldon Mossey caught up with her and grabbed her arm. "What are you doing? He said he'd kill her if we follow."

For the first time since he'd appeared out of the woods, Thea got a good look at her mother's preacher. Maybe it was her imagination or maybe her job had made her overly suspicious, but it seemed to her now that his appearance was *carefully* unremarkable. A benign façade created to court trust and calm doubts. But behind the glasses, his eyes were a flinty bluish gray with a hint of hostility.

She glanced down where he clutched her arm before shaking him off. "Find a phone and call 9-1-1."

"You're still going after him?" he asked incredulously. "You're going to get her killed!"

"Find a phone! Now!"

He retreated with a reluctant nod. "If anything happens to her…"

Thea didn't wait around to hear the rest of his threat. She plunged into the trees, following a trail of snapped twigs and trampled underbrush. She tried to suppress the sound of her pursuit, but she didn't dare let Sway get too far ahead. Sooner or later, he'd have to let Taryn go. She'd only slow him down. The only question was whether Thea could catch up in time to save her.

The trees began to thin as they circled back toward Reggie's neighborhood. Sway must have left a vehicle parked somewhere nearby. Up ahead, she saw something on the ground. Then she recognized Taryn's white shirt and pale blond hair. She wasn't moving. As Thea closed in, she saw blood on the woman's hands where she clutched her throat.

Thea approached with caution, her gaze darting through the trees and underbrush. She knelt beside Taryn and felt for a pulse. Weak but steady. Her eyes fluttered open.

"Did you see where he went?" she rasped. "You have to go after him!"

"Shush. Don't try to talk," Thea said. "You're losing blood, so we need to get you to a hospital." She jerked her T-shirt over her head. She wore a sports bra beneath but modesty was the least of her worries. For the second time in as many days, she pressed a makeshift bandage to a wound to staunch the blood flow. The cut was about three or four inches long, though it didn't look deep enough to have damaged any major arteries or veins. Still, there was a lot of blood.

"Go after him!" Taryn rasped. "Don't let him get away!"

"We'll find him again, I promise. Right now, we need to make sure you're okay."

She clutched at Thea's arm. "I don't care what happens to me. Don't you understand? He knows where she is!" She struggled to sit up, but Thea pressed her down.

"Just lie still—"

"Please!"

Thea hesitated and then, putting herself in Taryn's place, nodded. "Keep pressure on the wound. Like this." She took Taryn's hand and pressed it against the T-shirt. "Don't let up until help comes, okay?"

Then she stood and, with one last glance at Taryn Buchanan, struck out in pursuit.

JAKE HAD BEEN operating in total darkness since surfacing from the pool, but now he noticed a flicker of light up ahead, so thin and faint as to be nothing more than an optical illusion. Or wishful thinking. But he wasn't imagining the draft against his wet skin or that strange hollow melody that came to him now and then like a ghostly warning.

He kept one hand on the damp limestone wall as he moved slowly but steadily toward that sliver of wavering light. He had no idea where it was coming from. Earlier, when he'd first emerged from the tunnel, he hadn't seen any other passageways in the cavern, but maybe he'd missed it somehow. Maybe his attacker had crawled into a tunnel and Jake was seeing the illumination of his flashlight or headlamp.

Could his team already be in the cave? He started to call out, wanted badly to call out, but what if his assailant still lurked nearby? Someone had hit him hard enough to daze him and then kicked him into the pool to drown. Whatever other delusions the blackness might conjure, Jake wasn't imagining the bump on his head or the pain in his ribs. Nor was he imagining the whisper of fresh air that drifted in from some hidden place.

He kept going, his hand feeling along the clefts and recesses in the limestone. The glimmer was coming from a narrow gap in the wall. As Jake shuffled closer, his feet bumped against a pile of crushed rock and debris on the floor. He bent and felt his way over the obstacles.

Except for the draft and that minuscule beacon, he detected nothing unusual about this corner of the cave. If the flickering light had been there before, he surely would have noticed it. But it was possible the faint illumination had become lost in the brighter beam of his flashlight. Also possible that the doll floating in the pool had already captured his attention.

Had he been in the cave long enough for the sun to shift position? If there was an opening to the outside, maybe that was why he could see the light now and not earlier. He didn't think he'd been belowground much more than an hour, two at the most, but the blow to his head could have distorted his perception. His predicament seemed so surreal that he actually wondered if he was still trapped in the vortex, unconscious and dreaming as he swirled into a sinkhole.

The needle stings in his palms from the jagged rock grounded him in reality. His heart quickened as he crawled over the debris and closed in on the quivering light. He put up a hand and the shimmer disappeared. He lowered his hand, letting the pinhole brightness tunnel back through the darkness. He could make out a two- or three-foot indentation in the wall from which a tunnel opened up from the side. This really was an optical illusion, he realized. The passage was invisible unless you crawled up inside the depression. The flickering light came from a crack in the wall at the rear of the cavity.

He could hear a steady drip of water somewhere nearby. Hunkering inside the depression, he peered into the mouth of the tunnel. As soon as he entered the passage, he would once more be exploring in complete blackness. The illumination in the alcove wasn't much, but it was something. Still, a wisp of fresh air on his face made him wonder if there was another way out of the cave through the tunnel.

He considered his options as he crouched in the recess. Check out the hidden passage or sit tight and wait for his team. He knew what he *should* do. But the niggle had returned to the back of his neck, prodding him forward until he realized he didn't have a choice, after all. As long as there was a chance—no matter how slim— that Kylie could be lost somewhere inside the cave, he would keep going regardless.

Cocking his head toward the sound of dripping water, he took a moment to steady his nerves. Then he crawled through the tunnel until he bumped up against a wall. Feeling his way with an outstretched hand, he turned right, maneuvering through a space so tight, he worried he might get stuck between the walls. After a few stomach-clenching moments, the tunnel widened and the darkness seemed to thin. Another right turn back toward the pool cavern and then several more yards on his belly and elbows. Up ahead, he saw another crack in the wall through which a brighter radiance emanated.

Squeezing through into a small cavern, he slowly rose with his hands overhead. He could stand in a stooped position. Reason told him Kylie could never have found her way back through the maze of tunnels. Nor was it likely that someone had carried her or even dragged her through the tight passages. He was down here wasting precious time. Still, he moved forward, turning once more to the right—and then suddenly the wavering illumination seemed to explode.

The light was so brilliant at first, he thought he must have emerged from the cave into full sunlight. Yet another illusion. The cavern was large, but he was still surrounded by limestone walls. When he lifted his head, he could feel the draft on his face. Somewhere above him, there was an opening to the surface where fresh air and a sliver of sunlight seeped in.

But the flickering light didn't come from the sun. Someone had been in the cavern moments before him and left candles burning in old wine bottles. That person might still be inside, Jake realized as he peered through the dancing shadows. Despite the fresh air from above, the relentless dribble of water down the limestone walls gave the place a dank, mildewy smell.

He appeared to be alone, but he wasn't taking any chances. He drew his weapon as he searched for another way out or even a fissure in the wall where his attacker might lurk. Judging by the faded graffiti on the walls and the rusty beer cans strewed across the floor, the cavern had once been used for clandestine parties.

If not for the lighted candles, Jake might have thought the place had gone untouched for decades. But someone had been inside just before him. Someone who knew the hidden grotto's dark secret.

The drip of water seemed to fade away as the pounding in his ears grew louder. He dropped his weapon to his side as he focused on another pile of dirt and rock. On the wall behind the heap, someone had painted a cross. Rather than randomly placed, the wax-covered wine bottles had been arranged around the mound like votive candles at an altar.

At one end of the old grave, a partially exposed skull peeked through the rubble.

Chapter Nine

"I just spoke with Eldon Mossey," Nash Bowden told Thea as they stood on the street in front of Reggie's house. "He's at the hospital with Taryn. Looks like she's going to be okay."

"That's a relief," Thea said. "But still no sign of Derrick Sway?"

Chief Bowden shook his head. "We've got officers sweeping the area and traffic stops on all the major roads. There's always a chance someone will spot him and call in."

"Let's hope so. He's not exactly the type to blend in." Thea combed fingers through her tangled ponytail in frustration. "I can't believe he got away. He didn't have that much of a lead on me. I could have sworn I was right behind him. For someone of his age and size, he moves fast. Makes me wonder if he was able to vanish so quickly because someone helped him."

"When you first got here, did you notice a vehicle parked on the street? Anyone that looked suspicious or out of place hanging around the neighborhood?"

"No, but I haven't lived here in years," she said.

"I don't know the neighbors or the cars they drive. A parked vehicle or even someone walking down the street wouldn't have stood out for me. Although I'm certain I would have noticed Derrick Sway."

They were going back over the same information Thea had already provided earlier to one of the responding officers. Both she and Eldon Mossey had given brief statements as the paramedics had loaded Taryn into an ambulance. Then Thea had gone back to Reggie's house to clean up and borrow a shirt. Once Nash Bowden arrived, he'd wanted to hear the details for himself.

He was a tall, serious man with a calm demeanor and brooding eyes. As they stood talking, she couldn't help thinking about Grace Bowden with her too bright smile and flashes of melancholy. Thea still suspected all was not well in the Bowden marriage—a notion that his ringless finger seemed to confirm—but a few minutes into her interview and any lingering questions about his character began to wane. She could see why Jake liked him.

"Don't beat yourself up over the Sway situation," he said. "He got away because you stopped to help Taryn. I would have done the same in your position. If not for your quick action, she might have suffered massive blood loss or worse before the paramedics arrived."

"I appreciate the kind words, Chief, but you're giving me far too much credit. The cut wasn't so deep as to be life-threatening. I'm sure she would have been fine regardless."

He seemed determined to cut her some slack. "You

couldn't have known that for sure. The important thing is she's alive."

"Yes, but I can't help wondering why Sway let her go. He could just as easily have killed her."

Bowden shrugged. "He bought himself some time. He knew if he wounded her, you'd stop to assist. If he'd killed her outright, you'd pursue."

"Which is exactly what I did, and I lost him anyway," Thea said. "He could be anywhere by now."

"He won't risk any of the main roads. My guess is he'll go to ground as soon as he's able. For all we know, he may have a hideout somewhere nearby. That could explain why you happened upon him in the woods. Anyone in his position with a lick of common sense would have already fled the area. There must be a reason he's sticking around here."

"He did say he has a score to settle with my mother," Thea said.

"What kind of score?"

"He didn't elaborate, only that he had a lot of scores to settle after ten years in prison. That's about all I got out of him. He didn't seem at all concerned about being caught, which makes me wonder again if he has someone helping him evade the police."

"It's possible. He was born and raised around here. He could still have friends in the area or someone he's coerced into helping him." Bowden paused, his dark gaze moving over the street. His casual attire—jeans, rolled-up sleeves and dusty black boots—belied the tenacious vigilance in his eyes. "Tell me again what he said about Kylie."

"That common sense should tell us she's either dead or halfway out of the country by now—an implication that she might have been trafficked. An associate of mine is keeping a close eye on the deep web sites we routinely monitor in case Kylie's photograph pops up."

He frowned. "What kind of sites?"

"Auction sites," Thea said.

He looked visibly shaken. "She's four years old."

"I've seen photographs of children even younger."

He swore under his breath. "How do you get any sleep at night?"

"I don't sleep well," Thea said. "I do my best to compartmentalize. Sometimes it works, sometimes it doesn't. I'm sure you have to do the same."

"Four years old." He looked sad and angry.

Thea understood only too well. "Sway sounded confident we wouldn't find her, but he never confessed to anything."

"Confession or not, he's our most viable suspect at this point." His features tightened resolutely.

"Maybe, but I got the feeling he enjoyed toying with me. Spouting things to try to set me off."

"You don't like him for the kidnapping?"

"I never said that. No, I agree with you. He's certainly a viable suspect." *And it's my fault he got away. I should have called for backup as soon as I saw him in the woods. I shouldn't have tried to take matters into my own hands.*

Aloud she said, "There's something else that worries me about my run-in with Sway. Agent Stillwell and I drove over here together earlier, but we split up.

I wanted to check on something in my mother's house and he left to search the woods. I haven't been able to reach him since. It's probably nothing. I'm sure he's just out of range or something. But after everything that happened with Sway…" She trailed off. "You can understand why I'm concerned."

Bowden gave her a puzzled look. "You don't know?"

A little tingle of fear worked its way up Thea's spine. "Know what?"

"He called in earlier to one of his agents. He heard a suspicious noise coming from the cave."

"What kind of noise?"

"Something that convinced him Kylie might be inside. He went down to check it out."

Thea's heart dropped. "He went in alone? People have died in that cave."

Bowden gave her another strange look. "His team and some of my officers are down there with him now. He's fine but…" An uncomfortable silence followed. For an experienced law enforcement officer, Nash Bowden didn't have a very good poker face.

"What happened?" Thea demanded. "Tell me."

"He found human remains in one of the caverns."

Anyone involved in child abduction cases dreaded hearing such news, and yet Thea realized she'd been steeling herself for the tragic possibility ever since she'd arrived in Black Creek. But he'd said "remains," not a body. Goose bumps prickled at the back of her neck. She took a gulp of air. "Not Kylie?"

He said with quiet emphasis, "I should have been clearer. He found *skeletal* remains."

Thea stared at him silently.

"The body was buried under a pile of rocks and debris in a remote area of the cave," he explained. "Whoever it is has been down there for years, possibly decades."

The implication punched through Thea's shock with the force of a physical blow, squeezing the air from her lungs in a painful rush. "Maya."

"That was my first thought," he admitted. "But we don't know anything for certain. The remains are only partially exposed. Agent Stillwell had the tunnel that runs back to the cavern sealed until a forensic anthropologist from Tallahassee can get here to oversee the excavation."

"When will that be?" Thea asked with a hitch in her voice. She swallowed and tried again. "We can't leave her down there indefinitely. We have to bring her up."

"We will, but the recovery has to be done right. You probably know better than I do that excavating skeletal remains is a delicate process."

"I know. I know. It's just…" She closed her eyes. "We've waited so long."

His gaze was kind. "I understand. I can't imagine what it's been like for you folks. I see Reggie in the diner now and then. Tough woman."

At the mention of her mother, Thea's heart sank even deeper. Reggie would have to be told sooner rather than later.

"I'm headed to the cave now, if you want to come along," Bowden said. "There's always the possibility that something may have been buried with the body that you or your mother will recognize. That could speed up the identification process. Barring that, we can test your DNA against the remains."

"I need to talk to Reggie before she hears about this from someone else," Thea said.

"I thought you might. Just so you know, we're trying to keep a lid on the news for as long as we can. Last thing we need is a bunch of sightseers getting in the way of the recovery efforts."

"I'll be discreet," Thea said. "So will Reggie."

"I didn't mean to imply otherwise. I just wanted to bring you into the loop. Anyway, I'll have one of my officers drive you to the hospital whenever you're ready."

"Thank you. But on second thought, I'd like to go out to the cave first." Thea would never be able to explain it so that it made sense to anyone else, but she felt the need to be close to her twin. Maya had been alone in that cave for nearly thirty years.

"We'll take the road," Bowden said. "It'll be faster than hiking through the woods."

BY THE TIME they got to the cave, the owner of the property had been notified and had arrived to unlock the gate. Thea assumed he was the elderly gentleman with white hair and stooped shoulders who watched the activity from the shade. She wondered what had run through his mind when he'd heard the news. Did he think this place was cursed? He'd erected a fence and posted warnings after the drowning deaths of two teenagers, when all the while another body—possibly that of a four-year-old girl—might already have been hidden deep inside the cave.

Two uniformed officers positioned between the boulders were gazing down into the pit. One of them bent to offer a hand as Jake emerged from the opening. When he saw Thea, he gave a little nod of acknowledgment before he turned to say something to the person coming up out of the cave behind him.

Chief Bowden left her to join the officers at the opening. For some reason, Thea hung back. She'd been eager to get here as quickly as possible, but now she felt strangely out of place as she observed the commotion around the cave entrance. She received a few deferential glances from some of the officers who recognized her. Their well-meaning attention took her back to the night Maya had gone missing and to the following terror-filled days when the whole community had turned out to look for her. Had she been this close all along? Had she died alone in a dank, hidden cavern crying out for her mama and Sissy?

"You okay?" Jake touched her elbow and she jumped. "Sorry. I thought you saw me come up."

His hair and clothing were wet and muddy, and there were scrapes on his hands and across both cheeks, most likely from crawling through close spaces.

Thea shuddered. "Jake, is it her?"

His voice was both soft and grim. "I'm sorry I wasn't the one to tell you. I did try to call—"

"It's okay. Just tell me now."

"We don't know. The skull is only partially exposed. Until the grave is excavated, we won't know if the rest of the skeleton is even intact. Predation and the damp environment will have taken a toll."

"How long do you think the excavation will take?" Her voice sharpened in a way she hadn't meant it to. She didn't want to take her nerves and impatience out on Jake.

If he noticed, he didn't let on. He glanced over at the pit. "Under these conditions? Your guess is as good as mine. Getting all the equipment back to that cavern will be tricky. It's a tight squeeze in places." He rubbed his elbow. "Once everything is in place, the tedious work begins. The area will need to be gridded and the dirt sifted one screen at a time. It's time-consuming for a reason. The bones and artifacts have to be meticulously labeled and cataloged. After so many years, we only have one shot at getting it right."

The implication stunned her, though she wasn't sure why. "Are you saying the cavern is a crime scene and not just a place where the body was dumped?"

"We don't know that, either. But we can't take the chance that a minute piece of evidence or DNA could be lost or overlooked out of carelessness or impatience. Something that might have the power to break the case wide open."

"After twenty-eight years," Thea said.

"After twenty-eight years."

"Justice." She said the word softly, but her voice was gritty with emotion.

He nodded, his jaw set with the same determination. But he said nothing else, giving Thea the opportunity to catch her breath. She'd noticed the abrasions on his face and arms and the wet, muddy clothing straight away, but now she saw something in his eyes that shook her—the look of a person who'd come too close to death. She'd experienced an inkling of that back in the woods with Derrick Sway, but this seemed different.

He must have seen something in *her* eyes because, just like that, a mask dropped, closing her off before she could probe too deeply.

Don't do that, she wanted to tell him. *Don't shut me out. Let me in.*

But he'd already turned his attention back to the pit where a uniformed officer had just emerged. "We'll try to get as much done as we can before Dr. Forrester and her team get here," Jake said in a matter-of-fact voice. "We're setting up a harness and pulley system at the entrance and placing battery-powered lanterns throughout the passageways and caverns. The one thing we have in our favor is that we don't have to worry about losing the light on the surface. Belowground, there is no night or day."

Thea nodded. "When do you think she'll be here?"

"Sometime this afternoon, if all goes well. She agreed to drop everything, but we're still in for a long wait before we'll know anything conclusive. Maybe you should head over to the hospital and talk to your mother. Let her know what's going on."

"Yes, I intend to, but I wanted to come here first." Thea folded her arms around her middle as if she could calm the fluttery sensation in the pit of her stomach. She was hardly a novice to recovery operations, but no experience or training had prepared her for this eventuality. After decades of waiting, she hadn't expected the discovery of her sister's remains to hit her so hard. "I need to go down there, Jake."

He looked worried. "I don't think that's a good idea. It's a hard scrabble through some of those passageways."

"I'm not claustrophobic. I can handle it."

"Under ordinary circumstances, I'd agree. But you were in a serious car accident yesterday. You admitted only this morning that you're not at the top of your game."

"I don't need you to protect me," she snapped.

"When have you ever? Being down there…" He lifted a hand to the back of his neck. "It's weird. It can mess with your head even under the best of circumstances."

Foreboding crept in as she wondered again about that look in his eyes. "I don't care. I need to go down there. I need to be with her. And yes, I'm well aware of how unreasonable that sounds, but I can't help it. It's how I feel."

"We don't even know if it's her," he said. "You should be prepared for that possibility, too."

"I still want to go in. And before you say anything else, let me point out that you're hardly in a position to lecture me about safety." She gave him a hard stare. "What were you thinking going down in the cave alone?"

He stared right back at her. "I was thinking that if Kylie was in there, frightened and possibly hurt, I'd never forgive myself if something happened to her in the space of time it took to get a crew out here. I was thinking that leaving her alone down there for even another second was too long. You would have done the same."

"That's exactly why I have to go down there. If the remains are Maya's, she's been alone in that cavern for twenty-eight years."

It wasn't even remotely comparable. He'd thought Kylie was still alive. Maya had been gone for a long time. She may have already been dead before her killer had carried her into the pitch-blackness of the cave. There was no rescuing her. No happy ending for her family.

Thea wanted to believe her sister had never experienced pain or loneliness or fear. She couldn't bear to think even now how Maya might have suffered. Year after year, there had been nothing Thea could do but wait and imagine. Now, finally, there was something she could do.

Jake lifted a hand and brushed back her hair. His touch both shocked and moved her, but she didn't want to react. Too many curious eyes were upon them. If she and Reggie had learned anything from all those years of side-glances and open stares, it was how to remain stoic in the face of unwanted attention. It only occurred to her later that her stoicism had shut Jake out, too.

He dropped his hand to his side. "I can tell you feel strongly about this."

"I do."

"Then I'll take you down there myself. We're trying to limit the number of people in the cave at a time, so it may be a little while."

"I can wait. Jake..." She resisted the urge to touch his

arm in spite of all those curious eyes. "I need to ask you something and I want you to tell me the truth. Something else happened down there, didn't it? I can see it in your eyes. I'm guessing that's why you're all wet."

"It's damp and muddy in some of the passageways."

She wasn't buying it. "Your clothes are soaked. You may as well tell me what happened. I'll find out sooner or later."

Reluctantly, he took her arm and led her away from the opening where they could speak in private. "We're not releasing a statement about this yet."

"You know you can trust me. What is it?"

"About a mile or so back in the cave, an underground river flows up into a pool in one of the caverns. I found a doll floating on the surface. It matches the description of the doll that was taken with Kylie."

"Oh my God."

He glanced away, studying the activity back at the cave. "We've got divers on the way."

"That's why I can't go in right now," Thea said. "You should have told me. Of course, I'll stay out of the way. Unless there's something I can do to help."

"No, trust me, this is a job for professionals. We just need to give them room to do their thing. I'll go in with you as soon as we're clear."

"That doesn't even matter anymore. Nothing matters now except finding Kylie. She could still be alive. A doll floating on the pool doesn't prove anything. Three percent, Jake."

He nodded wearily. "I'm not giving up, but the cave is a maze. Dozens of passageways and dead ends, and

I only made it about halfway through. Combing back through all those tunnels will eat up at least another day. I can't help wondering if that doll was put there as misdirection. A way to tie up our resources and manpower until it's too late."

"Maybe, but how would anyone know you'd go down there and find it?" Thea asked.

"No one could know for certain, but it was a good bet the cave would be searched more thoroughly after the initial canvass."

"What about the sound you heard earlier? Chief Bowden said that's why you went down in the first place."

"I don't know what I heard. Or who I heard." He ran fingers through his wet hair, a physical sign of his frustration. "I very much doubt it was Kylie."

Something in his tone alarmed her. "What do you mean?" Then, "You never said why your clothes are all wet."

"While I was trying to fish the doll out of the pool, someone came from behind and hit me over the head hard enough to daze me. Next thing I know, I'm caught in a whirlpool several feet below the surface. I lost my flashlight, so I was spun around underwater in complete darkness. No up, no down." He paused. "For a while there, I wasn't sure how I'd get out."

Thea watched his expression as he spoke. He still seemed shaken from the experience. She'd never seen him like that. "I knew something bad must have happened."

He summoned a brief smile. "I know what you're

thinking. I even thought so myself at the time. So much for my keen instincts. Someone came up behind me and I never sensed a thing."

"That's not what I'm thinking."

"No?"

"I'm thinking you could have died down there and I would never have known what happened to you."

"Thea." He said her name so softly she might have thought the tender missive was nothing more than a breeze sighing through the treetops.

The sun bearing down on them was hot and relentless, but Thea felt a little shiver go through her. It hit her anew how much she'd missed that tender glint in his eyes as their gazes locked. How much she'd missed his husky whispers in the dark. The glide of his hand along her bare skin, the tease of his lips and tongue against her mouth. The way he had held her afterward, as if he never wanted to let her go. But he had let her go and she'd done nothing to stop him.

She drew a shaky breath. "Don't ever do that to me again."

"Get caught in a whirlpool? I'll do my best."

She scowled at him. "Don't make light. You know what I mean."

"I'm fine, Thea." He seemed on the verge of saying something else, but he held back. Maybe he thought she wanted his restraint. She did, didn't she? They were in a precarious situation. Adrenaline and attraction could be a dangerous combination. Throw in unresolved issues and they were asking for trouble.

She flexed her fingers to try to release the pent-up tension. "You didn't catch a glimpse of your attacker?"

"It's pitch-black down there even with a flashlight. You can only see what's directly in front of you."

"Could it have been Derrick Sway? I had a run-in with him in the woods earlier. I'll tell you about it later, but I don't want to get sidetracked."

"Yes, I heard about that run-in from some of the officers before you arrived." A shadow flickered across his expression. "From the sounds of it, things got tense."

"You could say that. I'm trying to figure out if he had time to attack you in the cave and then swing through the woods and come up behind me on the trail."

"Aside from the timeline, Sway's a big guy. He might have a hard time in some of the narrow passages." Jake paused. "I thought at first the assailant must have followed me into the cave, but I was wrong. He or she was already inside. That's how I stumbled upon the remains. I noticed a flickering light through a crack in the rock wall."

"A flickering light?"

"Yes. Whoever was down there lit candles and left them burning in the cavern."

"How strange," Thea said with a pensive frown. "Why would someone leave lighted candles?"

"I have my suspicions." He seemed hesitant to finish his thought. "Whoever was down there obviously didn't want to be seen in the cave. He hit me over the head and pushed me off the ledge, hoping the whirlpool would suck me under. But even with me out of commission, he had to figure backup was already on the way. He fled without taking the time to crawl back to the cavern and snuff out the candles. I doubt he had any idea the light could be seen through a crack in the wall."

Dread seeped in despite Thea's best efforts. "I don't want to say it out loud... I hate to even think it."

"Go on."

"Do you think he was down there to dispose of another body?"

Jake glanced away. "I'd be lying if I said I hadn't considered that possibility."

"Maybe he intended to bury her in the same cavern where you found the remains, but when he heard you in another part of the cave, he had to improvise. I know I said finding Kylie's doll in the pool doesn't prove anything, but we can't discount the evidence."

"Which is why we have divers on the way." He had one eye closed as he tracked a hawk against the sun. Now he glanced back at Thea.

"You're holding back," she said. "Something else happened that you don't want to tell me."

"It may be nothing."

"Tell me," she insisted. "If Maya's remains are in that cavern, I have a right to know everything you found."

He glanced away before he nodded. "There was something strange about those candles."

"How so?"

He paused to consider his answer. "It seemed to me they were arranged ceremonially around the mound, as if it were an altar or...something. It sounds a little out there, but that's the impression I had."

She stared at him in horror. "Are you saying he came

back down into the cave to specifically visit the remains? To *use* them in some kind of ceremony or ritual?"

Jake shrugged, but his expression remained sober. "We're assuming the suspect is male because of the profile. But we don't even know that for certain."

Male or female, what kind of monster would come back after all this time to desecrate the grave of a four-year-old victim? The imagery shook Thea.

"We're dealing with a very sick mind, Jake."

"So it would seem." His expression turned regretful. "Maybe I shouldn't have told you about the candles. It's all conjecture at this point."

"No. Don't keep secrets. The not knowing has always been the hardest part. The things that go through your head…" She paused. "I never imagined *this*."

"Let's wait until after the excavation to draw conclusions. In the meantime, you have my word I'll tell you everything I know as soon as I know it."

"Thank you."

"For what?"

"For your candor. For finding her."

"We don't—"

"I know. But if it is her…do you have any idea what this means to us? All these years, we never knew where she was or what had happened to her. To think she was right here all along. So near I should have heard her calling out to me."

He seemed at a loss. "I don't know what to say."

"It's all right. Neither do I."

Their gazes clung for a moment longer before Jake said, "Do you want to take a walk?"

That surprised her. "A walk? Where to?"

"There's something I need to check out. I'd like you to come with me, but it could be a hike. I noticed you were limping back at the station."

"I'm fine. Just a superficial cut on my heel. I hardly feel it now. But, Jake, don't you want to be here when the divers arrive?"

"This won't take long. If my hunch is correct, I think you'll want to see this," he said mysteriously.

Chapter Ten

Jake spoke to the property owner before he and Thea set out. Douglas McNally could give him only a vague sense of where an opening might be over the hidden cavern. He claimed he'd never known of a second cave entrance and clearly thought searching for one in his rocky field a waste of time. However, Jake had felt fresh air in the tunnel, and he'd glimpsed a sliver of sunlight through the limestone roof. Whoever had attacked him at the pool, and left burning candles around the grave, might well have exited through that opening or another one nearby.

One of Jake's team members had loaned him a phone so that he could stay in touch until he could get a replacement. He glanced at the screen now to first check the time and then the compass. They were still on course as far as he could tell. Strange to think that the cave ran beneath their feet. Stranger still to hike through their pastoral surroundings when only a short while ago he'd been trapped in a subterranean whirlpool, fighting for his life in pitch-blackness. The sunlight and song-birds seemed to mock his close call.

"From the Devil's Pit the cave runs south," Mr. Mc-Nally had told him. "Then it slants slightly eastward before you get to the final dead end. Head off in that direction. If there is another entrance, you might get lucky and stumble across it. But I wouldn't get my hopes up. As far as I know, there's only ever been one way in and one way out. I'd tell you again that you're wasting your time, but I can see you're determined. Besides, it's possible rain and erosion have carved out another opening since I last went exploring. Wouldn't surprise me if that old cave has a few more secrets to give up."

Yes, maybe it does, Jake thought. He wanted to believe they were getting close to a break in the case, but even with his experience, he could still be susceptible to wishful thinking. Forty-eight hours and counting since Kylie Buchanan had been reported missing. Spirits had visibly flagged back at the cave while they'd waited for the divers. Jake had sensed despondency and an unnerving sense of calm, as if they were no longer working against the clock. The discovery of Kylie's doll in the pool and the skeletal remains in the cavern were somber reminders of how many abducted children never came back home.

He slanted a glance at Thea as they walked along the rough terrain. She'd been quiet since they'd left the others.

She sensed his gaze and returned his scrutiny. "You're still not going to tell me where we're going?"

"To be honest, I'm not sure. But I'll know it when we get there."

"Always so cryptic." She stopped in the shade of a pine tree to tie her shoe.

He gave her a worried frown. "Are you sure you're up to this? I know you must be in pain. You didn't exactly walk away from that crash without a scratch." He searched her upturned face, noting the cuts and bruises that were more pronounced today than yesterday, and the circles under her eyes that seemed to have darkened since earlier that morning. "Wait for me here if you need to."

"I'm just a little winded." She finished with her laces and stood. "Guess I've been sitting behind a computer screen for too long."

"Yes, I've been meaning to talk to you about your career choices." He tried to lighten the mood with a joke.

"Some other time." She idly toed a pine cone out of the way. "Actually, I didn't really need a breather. I stopped because we need to talk about what happened in the woods earlier."

She had his undivided attention. "With Sway? I'm all ears."

"You said you heard things got tense. That's an understatement." She gave him a quick summary of the drawing she'd found on Reggie's refrigerator, the subsequent confrontation with Sway, and how the situation had escalated with him on the run and Taryn Buchanan in the hospital.

"But she's going to be okay," Jake said when Thea paused.

"No thanks to me. There's no excuse for my behavior. I should have called in the minute I spotted Sway on the trail. Instead, I lost control of the situation. I'm lucky I didn't get someone killed."

"Why didn't you make that call?" Jake asked.

She cringed. "It sounds stupid now, but in the back of my mind, I thought I could get him to talk because of his previous relationship with Reggie. It was never going to happen. He led me to believe he'd reveal something about Maya, but all he did was play me. What I can't figure out is why he forced the confrontation in the first place. He said he mistook me for Reggie from a distance—you were right about a grudge, by the way—but I think he had another agenda."

"Maybe he was trying to keep you away from the cave."

"That's possible. He had mud on his jeans and boots, and he's certainly capable of violence. We shouldn't underestimate him, Jake. He's strong and he moves quickly and quietly for a man of his size and age. I can imagine him sneaking up behind you in the dark." She paused on a shiver. "He has the usual prison ink, but also occult imagery on his neck and arms. It's not a stretch to think he could have been the one to place the candles around the remains."

"Scary dude," Jake said.

"He is." Thea paused again. "It's odd. When Taryn and Eldon Mossey showed up, Sway could have used the distraction to try to disarm me. He could have easily overpowered me. Instead, he just stood there and waited. Maybe his plan all along was to provoke Taryn into attacking him, but how could he know she'd react so viscerally?"

"She's the mother of a missing child. Not that difficult to predict her behavior."

"I guess. The whole time I had my gun on Sway, I had the feeling that I'd interrupted something. I couldn't help wondering if he'd gone into the woods to meet Eldon Mossey."

"That's jumping to a big conclusion," Jake said. "Especially since Mossey and Taryn were in the woods together. A meeting seems risky unless you think she was there to meet Sway, as well."

"I don't. Not after I witnessed her reaction to him. However Eldon Mossey may be involved, I don't think Taryn had anything to do with Kylie's disappearance."

"Because she attacked Sway?"

"Because she was desperate for me to go after him regardless of what happened to her. The whole thing went down so quickly it's possible I misread their interaction, but I don't think she and Eldon Mossey are as close as Reggie assumed. I got the distinct impression that Taryn didn't want anything to do with him. She kept shrugging his hand away when he tried to touch her."

"Yet she was out in the woods alone with him."

"At this point, she'd probably accept help from the devil himself if he promised to find Kylie. We've been focused on Derrick Sway for obvious reasons, but I think we need to take a harder look at Eldon Mossey. You said yesterday the information you have on him is sketchy. Have you learned anything else?"

"Nothing concrete, but there is one piece of information that may be significant," Jake told her. "His father was also a preacher. He used to lead a prison ministry group out of his church in Butler, Georgia. According to some of the former congregation, the elder Mossey died about ten years ago. Eldon continued the ministry for a while but he moved away a few years after his father passed. The church has since burned down, and no one seems to know where Eldon went or what he was doing until he turned up in Black Creek."

Thea swung around. "Could he have met Sway through this ministry? If they kept in touch, he would have known when Sway got out of prison. In fact, Sway could be the reason Eldon came to Black Creek in the first place."

"I can request Sway's call and visitation recordings from the prison, excluding any communication with his attorney, of course. If the facility still has copies of his jail mail, we can get a court order to look through his incoming and outgoing correspondence. But all that takes time. Meanwhile, I've asked the Macon office to keep digging around in Mossey's hometown. I'll let you know if anything else turns up."

Thea shaded her eyes as a shaft of sunlight slanted across her face. "Why didn't you tell me about this earlier at the police station?"

"It didn't seem particularly relevant until you mentioned a possible meeting in the woods with Sway. Mossey's ministry operated in Georgia. Derrick Sway was incarcerated in Florida. A connection between the two seemed unlikely."

"It's still a long shot," Thea conceded. "It's also possible I imagined the vibe I picked up between them.

But I'm not wrong about Eldon Mossey. There's something off about him. He's just a little too ordinary, if you know what I mean."

"I know exactly what you mean. It's like he's purposely cultivated an image that allows him to fade into the woodwork. You'd glimpse him on the street and forget about him."

"Yet both my mother and Grace Bowden seem captivated by him."

Jake said in surprise, "The chief's wife? What does she have to do with Eldon Mossey?"

"Apparently she attends the same church as Reggie. She said Brother Eldon's sermons are so riveting that she sometimes forgets to pay attention to anyone else in attendance."

"That's quite a testimonial."

"Reggie said all the young people in the church adore him."

"This guy," Jake muttered.

"Sounds a little too good to be true, doesn't he?"

"I'm beginning to think so, but we'll need more than gut instinct to get a warrant. At the very least, we can bring him in for another chat."

Thea kicked aside a pine cone in a burst of frustration. "Why did I let Derrick Sway escape? If he took Kylie and we don't find him in time—"

"It won't be your fault."

"It's hard not to think so."

"Let it go," Jake advised. "I've been where you are, and it does no one any good to obsess over what you could have done differently. We need to stay focused."

She glanced at him. "Then give me something to do. Let me help you."

"We'll talk about it later, after you've seen Reggie. Right now, let's keep moving."

They set out again with Jake periodically checking his compass. Cabbage palms dotted the rocky landscape, along with clumps of pine trees and southern red cedars. The temperature climbed steadily until Thea stopped again to fan her face.

"Maybe I really am out of shape."

"The humidity is killer," Jake said. "And you did get pretty banged up yesterday."

"I can't keep using the wreck as an excuse. I need to hit the gym hard when I get back to DC."

Jake gave her a sidelong glance. "Maybe you need a workout partner. You used to kick my ass on the stair mill."

"Beating you was serious motivation." She was only half teasing.

"Ever wonder if I let you win?"

"No. The thought never crossed my mind. And it better not have crossed yours."

How easy it was to slip back into their old banter, Jake thought. He would have liked nothing better than to sit in the shade and spend the rest of the day talking about unimportant things with Thea. But they were serious people with a serious job to do. If they were lucky, a lighter moment might come later.

"Come on," he said, "we're almost there. I can feel it."

No sooner had the prediction left his lips than a breeze swept down through a massive live oak, stirring the Spanish moss that hung almost to the ground. With the breeze came the eerie hollow melody that Jake had heard first in the woods behind Reggie's house and then from inside the cave.

Thea turned toward the sound. "Do you hear that? Reminds me of the wind chime in Grace Bowden's courtyard."

"We're definitely getting close," he said.

She looked slightly alarmed. "Close to what?"

"When I heard the sound earlier, I thought it was coming from inside the cave. Now I think it must have been coming from up here. There has to be an opening in the ground where air and sound seeps down into the tunnels." He moved away from her, searching along the uneven terrain. "Keep an eye out. The entrance could be small and covered over by rocks and scrub brush."

She remained in place, her head still tilted toward the sound. "You heard this all the way down in the cave? That must have been creepy."

"Close your eyes for a moment and you'll get some idea."

"No thanks," she said with an exaggerated shudder.

Jake moved quickly up the slope, searching through the trees and bushes and all along the rocky summit. Even with his eyes peeled, he almost missed the narrow opening, camouflaged as it was by brush and boulders. Only a child or a very small adult could squeeze through the fissure. He doubted whoever had been in the cave had climbed up the limestone wall and exited the cave that way.

High up in one of the trees, a wooden wind chime

had been hung to either mark the opening to the cave or the hidden grave below. Or both. The chime was old and weathered. The hollow tubes had been strung together on fishing line. Some of them had rotted and fallen to the ground. Enough remained intact, however, to create a haunting melody when the wind blew through the treetop.

Jake turned to call to Thea, but she was right behind him, her eyes riveted on the ground. "Do you see them?" she asked in a hushed voice.

"See what?"

She dropped to her knees and began to paw frantically through a patch of wild rosemary, releasing a pungent scent reminiscent of camphor. He hunkered beside her, mesmerized by her frenzy. Then he saw them and leaned in to take a closer look.

Hidden beneath the vegetation, two primitive stick figures had been etched into the surface of a flat rock partially buried in the ground near the opening.

BY THE TIME they arrived back at the main entrance, the divers had arrived and were checking their tanks and equipment before they entered the cave. The operation would take hours, and as much as Thea wanted to stay, she couldn't put off her visit with Reggie any longer. Once people started to notice the activity to and from Mr. McNally's property, curiosity seekers would eventually show up at the cave. Word would get out about Jake's discoveries. Reggie shouldn't have to hear about either from anyone but her daughter.

Jake gave her the keys to his SUV and promised

to get in touch as soon as he knew anything. Hot and tired, Thea hitched a ride back to Reggie's place with one of the uniformed officers. Thankfully, he wasn't in a chatty mood, so the trip passed quietly, giving her a few minutes to think and catch her breath.

Her mind wandered back to the cave. She couldn't help dwelling on those lighted candles placed around the remains and the stick figures carved into the surface of the rock like a headstone. Two stick figures that mimicked Maya's artwork and were reminiscent of the twin totems Jake had found in the woods. What did those crude renderings symbolize? The answer seemed obvious—two figures, two sisters. But only Maya had been taken. Had the kidnapper meant to take Thea that night, as well? Maybe his plan had been to carry the twins away one at a time, but for some reason his second trip had been thwarted. If Thea hadn't climbed into Maya's empty bed, she might well have been the first to be taken.

Think! What do you remember about that night?

She summoned memories she couldn't be sure were even real. They *seemed* real. So vivid she could feel the breeze from the open window on her face. She could hear muted laughter and music from the front porch, and the eerie sound of a neighbor's dog baying in the woods. Something else. A sound that mingled with the bullfrogs and cicadas.

I'm scared, Sissy.

Why?

I heard something.

It's just a coonhound out in the woods. See? Mama opened the window.

It's not a coonhound.

"Agent Lamb?"

She roused at the sound of her name. She glanced at the officer and then at her surroundings. They were sitting behind Jake's SUV in her mother's driveway. For a few moments there, she'd lost track of time and place.

She gave the officer a sheepish smile. "Sorry. I must have drifted off."

"I thought you were awfully quiet over there. You need anything before I go?"

"No, I'm fine. Thanks for the ride."

"No problem."

She climbed out of the car and watched as he backed out of the driveway. He gave her a little salute as he straightened the wheel and stepped on the gas. After a moment, the sound of the car engine died away, leaving the street empty and quiet. So much had happened since she'd left the hotel earlier that morning to look for coffee. She almost wished she could go back in time and pull the covers over her head.

Lingering at the edge of the driveway, she glanced up and down the street. Was Derrick Sway still in the area? Was he hunkered down somewhere nearby, waiting for his chance to get to Reggie? To get to her?

As preoccupied as she was by what had been found in the cave, now was not the time to lower her guard. She wanted to believe Sway would have the good sense not to accost her twice in one day, but he'd made it clear earlier that he had no fear of being caught. After

ten years in one of the most dangerous correctional fa-
cilities in the state, she doubted there was anything he
did fear.

Had he taken Maya and then returned twenty-eight
years later to abduct Kylie? Had he hung the totems in
the woods to taunt Reggie? To make her suffer for the
ten years he'd spent behind bars?

Thea scanned the backyard through the chain-link
fence and peered into the shadowy recesses between the
outbuildings. She searched along the side of the house
and across the front porch. Up and down the street once
more, and into shadowy yards and behind windows.

Are you watching me?

Yes, the wind seemed to whisper.

She tried to rein in her imagination, but a person
didn't go through what she'd experienced at a tender
age and come out unscathed. No one could hunt mon-
sters by day, even from the safety of a computer screen,
and sleep peacefully ever again. She knew what was
out there.

Sweeping the street one last time, she turned her
back on the row of modest homes and crossed the
yard to the porch. The back of her neck prickled as
she climbed the steps slowly, but she resisted the urge
to glance over her shoulder. No one was there. No one
that she could see.

Letting herself in the front door, she pocketed the
key rather than return it to the flowerpot. Someone had
apparently been coming and going as they pleased. She
wasn't about to make it easy for them.

The house had a different smell this time. The fresh

air from the open bedroom window had removed the fusty odor she'd noticed earlier, but now she detected something faintly medicinal. Eucalyptus maybe or camphor. It reminded her a little of the wild rosemary that had covered the etching on the flat stone. Had someone been in here while she'd been exploring with Jake?

Drawing her weapon, she walked across the room and checked the kitchen. Maya's artwork was still on the table where she'd left it. Thea studied her sister's creation for a split second before she whirled and made her way along the hallway.

She wouldn't have been surprised to hear the eerie clacking of a wooden wind chime somewhere nearby. Already she'd come to associate that hollow melody with the disappearances. Whoever had left the totems in the woods had years earlier marked the spot of Maya's grave by etching stick figures onto the surface of a rock and hanging wind chimes from a tree branch. Then her killer had gone back to visit the remains and to light candles in a ritual that only he could understand.

There must be some significance to that sound, Thea thought. A clue hiding in plain sight that had eluded her for twenty-eight years.

She went into her old bedroom and made certain the window was closed and locked. Then she did the same throughout the house. When she let herself out the front door, she noticed a man circling Jake's SUV as he peered through the tinted windows. He was tall and lanky, with the nonchalant demeanor of someone unafraid of getting caught or standing out. Probably a neighbor, Thea decided. A bluetick reclined in the shade a few feet from the driveway.

She called out to the man as she came down the steps. "Can I help you?"

The hound dog opened his eyes and flapped his tail lazily, but he didn't get up.

The man came around to the front of the vehicle and leaned an arm against the hood. "Saw you over here. Thought you might know what happened to the fellow that drives this Suburban."

"What makes you think anything has happened to him?" Thea strode across the yard, mindful of her weapon tucked beneath the tail of her borrowed T-shirt. Now that she had a closer look at the interloper, she recognized Reggie's across-the-street neighbor. The familiarity did nothing to quell her caution. Instead, her nerve endings prickled a warning. Reggie had never made any bones about her dislike of Lyle Crowder. Thea tried to remember why as she closed the distance between them. *It's creepy the way he sits over there on his front porch staring across the street at our house. Probably peeps in our windows while we're asleep at night.*

"I couldn't help noticing that his vehicle has been parked in the driveway all morning. Reggie's not home, so it struck me as odd." He paused to give Thea a closer scrutiny. "She know you're here?"

"I'm her daughter."

He squinted and straightened. "You're Reggie's girl? Damn, I never would have known you. You don't look like I remember."

"It's been a minute," Thea said. "How've you been, Mr. Crowder?"

"No need for the 'mister' part. We've been neighbors since you were yay high." He bent to measure the air a few feet from the ground. "How long you in town for?"

"I haven't decided."

Lyle Crowder had changed, too, Thea noted. He'd grown older, grayer and a good deal thinner. He seemed friendly enough, but she couldn't dismiss the lingering unease from Reggie's contempt. *If he ever comes over here when I'm not home, you go inside and lock the door. Don't even think about letting him come inside.*

A thrill skittered up Thea's spine but she kept her expression neutral.

"I heard about Reggie's car accident," he said. "She okay?"

"Her injuries are serious, but she'll recover."

"Glad to hear it. My buddy owns the junkyard where they towed her old car. He said it was a real mess. Said she's lucky to be alive."

While he spoke, Thea cataloged his appearance as she had earlier with Derrick Sway. Cargo shorts, paint-stained T-shirt and flip-flops. His hair was damp from sweat or a recent shower. She thought of Jake's close call in the cave and wondered if Lyle Crowder would have had time to hightail it back home and clean up while they'd searched for the second entrance. Crawling through tight passageways would certainly explain the scratches on his arms and shins.

"Any idea when she'll get to come home?"

Thea forced her mind back to the present conversation. "Probably by the end of the week. I'll be sure to tell her you asked about her."

She watched his expression. He nodded as if he didn't have a care in the world, but something ambiguous glinted in the depths of his eyes.

"Have you noticed anyone or anything suspicious in the neighborhood this morning?" Thea asked.

"Heard a gunshot earlier. That's not so unusual around here. Some of the local boys like to shoot beer cans in the woods. But the sirens caught my attention. Cop cars and an ambulance. Do you know if they found the little girl?"

Which one?

"I'm afraid not," Thea said. "You haven't noticed anyone hanging around Reggie's house, have you? Or seen anyone go into or come out of the woods?"

"No, but I was working out back most of the morning, digging up some old blackberry vines and whatnot. Thorns got me good." He examined a long scratch on his forearm. "You say they haven't found her yet, but something must have happened, else why all those sirens?"

"Do you know a man named Derrick Sway?"

The name seemed to give him pause. Then he gestured toward the SUV. "I was just telling the FBI agent about him yesterday."

"Agent Stillwell?"

"That's the one. Was I right? Did Sway have something to do with little Kylie's disappearance?"

"We don't know that yet. He's certainly a person of interest," Thea said. "We think he may be hiding out somewhere in the area. If you see him in the neighbor-hood, we'd appreciate a call to the police."

"Don't have to tell me twice. That guy's always been bad news in my book. Smartest thing your mama ever did was giving him the boot."

Thea couldn't disagree.

"Speaking of…" Crowder said, still with that curious glint. "I'd keep an eye on Reggie if I were you. Could be nothing more than rumors, but I hear Sway's got it in for her. You cross a guy like that, he'll get even sooner or later."

"She's well protected in the hospital," Thea assured him.

He nodded and glanced away. "Good to know."

The hound got up and wandered over to rub against Crowder's leg. He reached down and scratched behind the dog's ears. "This here's old Blue. Not much of a hunter these days, but still good company."

As if on cue, the dog plopped down on a shady patch of grass and closed his eyes, oblivious to the squirrel hopping from branch to branch above him.

"Didn't you have a bluetick hound years ago?" Thea asked. "This can't be the same one." Was it Crowder's dog that had been baying in the woods the night Maya had been taken?

"I've had a few over the years," he said. "Always did love a good coonhound."

"I seem to recall you worked away from home a lot. What happened to your dogs when you were gone?"

"I'd drop whichever one I had at the time at my brother's house and pick him up on the way home. That wouldn't work with Blue, though. He won't let me out of his sight."

"Do you ever take him into the woods?"

"Sometimes."

"Have you ever seen anything hanging from the trees?" Thea asked.

He looked startled. "Hanging from the trees? What in the hell are you talking about, girl?"

"I'm talking about dolls of a sort made from hollow pieces of wood with carved faces and twigs for arms and legs. Fabric hearts glued to the torsos and tufts of hair strung from the heads. If there's more than one, they sound a bit like bamboo wind chimes when they bump against each other in the breeze."

He said in a hushed voice, "You found something like that in *these* woods?"

"Yes, behind Reggie's house."

He glanced past her toward the backyard. He didn't strike Thea as the religious type, but she wouldn't have been surprised if he'd crossed himself. "What do you think it means?"

She shrugged. "I was hoping you could tell me."

He ran a hand up and down his arm as if trying to wipe away chill bumps. "I've never seen anything like that around here, but I witnessed plenty of weirdness when I worked on the rigs. Grown men carrying gris-gris pouches in their pockets and perforated dimes around their necks or ankles. Not that I didn't send up a prayer now and then myself. You need something to believe in when you're trapped out there at night with nothing but ocean for miles. Gets spooky as hell when the sun goes down. What you described sounds like a poppet."

"You've seen one?" Thea asked.

"A guy that worked on my crew found something similar under his pillow once. Crude thing. Looked liked it was made out of old rags and dirty yarn. This dude was crazy superstitious and a regular horndog to boot. We figured someone put it there as a joke, or maybe a jealous husband or boyfriend wanted to give him a scare. We ribbed him about it for days, but then he just up and disappeared one night. No one saw anything and nothing was caught on the security cameras. He was just gone. Never found so much as a trace."

"You think someone threw him off the platform?"

"Either that or something caused him to jump." Crowder stared down at his dog with a frown. "That's my one and only experience with voodoo, hoodoo—whatever you want to call it. But that sound you described? I don't think there's anything too spooky about that. Used to be an old widow woman out on the highway that made wind chimes and sold them on the side of the road. At first people bought them just to help her out, and then it became popular to hang them in trees for good luck. When the wind blew just right, you could hear the damn things all over town. You don't remember that?"

Thea shook her head.

"Before your time, I guess."

"Have you ever seen any of those chimes out in the woods?" she asked.

"Haven't seen them anywhere in years, but your

mama used to have some hanging from that big old oak tree in her backyard. I could hear them all the way across the street when a storm was coming in."

Thea was silent for a moment, deep in thought. Something else had come back to her. It wasn't just the dog that had awakened Maya that night. It was the sound of Reggie's wind chimes.

I'm scared, Sissy.

Why?

I heard something.

It's just a coonhound out in the woods. See? Mama opened the window.

It's not a coonhound, Sissy. Listen.

The dog had stopped baying and the music and laughter seemed to fade away as Thea lay on her back staring up at the ceiling. The wind chimes outside their window crackled loudly as if a shoulder had accidently brushed against them. Then the sound died away as a shadow moved across the ceiling.

"Somebody's out there," Maya whispered.

Thea shivered as she stared up at the shadow. "Nobody's out there," she whispered back. "Stop being a fraidy-cat and go back to sleep."

But somebody had been out there. Someone who had watched from the edge of the woods—or the safety of his front porch—before creeping across the backyard to climb through the open bedroom window.

Chapter Eleven

Thea showed her credentials to the guard outside Reggie's room and then lingered just inside the doorway. Her mother's head was turned toward the window. She lay so still that Thea assumed she was sleeping.

"Are you going to gawk at me all day or are you coming inside?" she grumbled, still with her head turned toward the window. Thea decided she must have seen her reflection in the glass.

"I thought you were sleeping. I didn't want to wake you." She moved to the foot of the bed, feeling awkward and at a loss. *You shouldn't feel that way at your own mother's bedside.* She couldn't help it. The discovery in the cavern painfully underscored the reason for their years of estrangement. "I'm sorry it took me so long to get here. How are you feeling?"

"Everything considered, I can't complain." Reggie pushed herself up against the pillows and adjusted her hospital gown. "How are you?"

"Me?" Thea shrugged. "I'm fine. Just a little sore is all."

Reggie searched her face. "Didn't get much sleep last night, did you?"

"No. But that's not unusual."

She frowned. "You need to take better care of yourself. You won't be young forever."

"I'm fine," Thea insisted as she idly smoothed her hand across the covers. "I need to talk to you about something."

"I'm not going anywhere," Reggie said.

Thea nodded absently. "The reason I'm late—"

"Oh, I know why you're late." Her mother's hard gaze tracked her as she came around to the side of the bed.

Thea said carefully, "What do you know?"

"You don't have to tiptoe around any of it. I know about Derrick Sway and what he did to poor Taryn." She paused. "I know what was found in that cave."

Thea released the breath she hadn't realized she'd been holding. Her heart had started to race despite her efforts to keep her emotions under control. "I'm sorry you had to hear about it from someone else. I should have come as soon as I found out, but I wanted to go to the cave first. I…needed to go to the cave. I needed to be close to her. I know how crazy that sounds—"

"No, it doesn't. Not to me. I would have done the same."

"Still, I'm sorry I wasn't the one to tell you," Thea said.

Reggie stared at her for a moment then lifted her chin in that stubborn way she had. "Doesn't matter how I found out. It's not her."

Thea stared back at her. "You can't know that for certain. You should prepare yourself. We both need to."

"It's not her." Reggie's blue eyes glittered like shattered glass. "Don't you think I would have known if my baby was that close? I'm telling you it's not her."

Thea sat on the edge of the bed. "But what if it is? At least we'll know. At least we can finally say our goodbyes. Don't you want closure?"

"Closure? How will that help anything?" Reggie balled her pale hands into fists on top of the covers. "You think we'll feel better if we can have a service and give her a headstone? All that will do is take away my hope." She turned her head back to the window. "As long as we don't know any different, she could still be alive. Someone good could have found her and taken her in. She could be happy with a family of her own by now. Don't you get it? She could still be alive."

Yes, now she got it. Thea put her hand over Reggie's. Her mother's face crumpled at the contact. "My poor baby."

"I know, Mama. I know."

She clutched Thea's hand. "Somebody buried her down in that awful place and left her there all these years." Her eyes spilled over. "I can't bear it. I don't care how many years have gone by, I can't stand to think of her alone and suffering. It's too much. No mother should ever have these images in her head. No child should ever have to suffer the way Maya did."

"And yet so many do," Thea said.

Reggie reached for a tissue. "I don't know how you do what you do. I truly don't. You got the short end of the stick when it comes to mothers, but just look at how you've turned out."

"I'm not sure what to say to that."

"Don't say anything." She placed her hand on Thea's arm. "Just let me get this out. Tomorrow everything will go back to the way it was, but right now I need you to know that no matter what happens or how many years go by, you'll always be my little girl."

Thea's throat tightened painfully. "Sometimes it seemed as if you didn't want me around anymore."

"I know. And you don't know how much I've come to regret that. I've thought about my behavior a lot over the years," Reggie said. "Why I withdrew from you the way I did. My only excuse is that I carried a lot of guilt on my shoulders. After what happened to Maya, I didn't think I deserved to be your mother. My misery was my punishment. That's why I stayed in Black Creek and put up with all the gossip and accusations even though we would have both been better off somewhere else. No matter what anyone said about me, it was never as bad as what I thought of myself. I just never stopped to consider that by staying here I was punishing you, too."

"That's all in the past," Thea said. "We can't go back and change things."

"No, and at least something good came from all that heartache. You help save kids like Maya every single day. She'd be so proud of her Sissy."

"I hope so." Self-conscious, Thea glanced away and, after a moment, Reggie released her hand. She sank back into the pillows, looking exhausted and unbearably fragile.

"Are you sure you're okay? Are you in pain?" Thea asked. "Physical pain, I mean."

"I'm okay. Doctor says I might be able to go home in a day or two." She didn't sound optimistic. Little wonder, Thea thought. Reggie was a trooper, but she'd been through hell in the past few days. A car wreck and surgery coming on the heels of another child's abduction would take the wind from anyone's sails.

"You're too thin." Thea voiced her worry. "You work too hard."

"I'm as strong as an ox," Reggie scoffed. "I can still sling hash with the best of them."

"I'm sure you can, but it's backbreaking work."

"It's all I know." She closed her eyes.

"Are you tired? Should I go?"

"You don't need to be so careful around me, Althea. And no, don't go. I like having you close."

"Then rest. I'll be right here," Thea said.

She used the ensuing silence to get up and hang her bag on the back of a chair. Glancing out the window, she thought how normal everything seemed three stories below. The sun was still shining. People hustled to and from the parking lot, while deep inside a cave a few miles away, divers searched an underground pool for a little girl's body.

"What's the weather like?" her mother asked.

Thea turned away from the window. "Hot and humid. Just as you would expect in Florida this time of year."

"I don't mind the heat," Reggie said. "It's the end of summer I can't bear."

"Why?" Thea walked over to the bed. "Cooler weather should be a welcome respite."

"Not for me. I don't like the end of things," her mother said. "I already dread the end of your visit."

"I'll try to be better about staying in touch."

"Don't make promises you won't keep."

"You could always come see me," Thea said.

Reggie gave her a half-hearted smile. "Maybe I will. That would surprise you, wouldn't it? Your old mama showing up on your doorstep."

"Yes," Thea replied candidly. "Give me some notice and I'll make your travel arrangements."

Reggie sighed. "It's a nice dream."

Thea sat on the edge of the bed again. "I hate to bring this up, but there's something else we need to talk about if you're up to it."

Reggie nodded. "You want to ask me about Derrick."

"How did you know?"

"It's all over the hospital what he did to Taryn. Lord only knows what would have happened if you hadn't been there to stop him."

"I didn't stop him," Thea said. "I'm just glad she's going to be okay despite my incompetence."

"She won't be okay until they find Kylie. Even then..." Reggie plucked at the blanket. "Anyway, what do you want to know about Derrick?"

"When was the last time you saw him?"

"Before he went to prison. He used to come into the diner and sit in my section so I'd have to wait on him. I could have switched tables with one of the other girls, but I didn't want to give him the satisfaction."

"You haven't seen him since he got out?"

"No, and up until today, I was grateful he'd kept his distance. We didn't exactly part on the best of terms."

"What happened between you? I never really knew," Thea said.

"I guess the short answer is that I came to my senses." She couldn't quite meet Thea's gaze. "I never should have taken up with him in the first place, but I always did have a thing for the bad boys. Even your daddy had a wild streak despite June's coddling." She paused, her brow wrinkling as she thought back. "After Maya went missing, I cut a lot of people out of my life. Not just Derrick, but friends I'd known for years. Some of them didn't want anything to do with me anyway, what with all the gossip and suspicion."

"What about your suspicions?" Thea asked. "Did you think Derrick had something to do with Maya's disappearance?"

Reggie seemed uncharacteristically reluctant to speak her mind.

"Just between you and me," Thea coaxed.

"Of course, I thought about it, but there was never anything connecting him to her abduction. Not that evidence or motive mattered to some. So many people around here made up their minds about me as soon as they heard the news." Her eyes burned into Thea's. "You've had your doubts at times. Don't bother denying it. I've seen it on your face."

Thea started to refute Reggie's accusation but then decided to come clean. Get everything out in the open. "I'll admit there's something I've always wondered about. Why didn't you tell the police you came back into our room that night to open the window?"

Reggie stared at her in confusion. "What?"

"In your official statement, you said the window was open because it was hot inside the house. That was true. But you never mentioned that you made a special trip to our room to open it after you'd put us to bed."

Reggie looked stumped. "Why does it matter when I opened the window?"

Because it does. "I'm just curious."

A shadow darkened her mother's eyes but she didn't turn away. She gazed at Thea without flinching. "You think I came back to open the window for the kidnapper?"

"No, of course not. I just—"

"Don't lie. Tell me the truth." Reggie grabbed her arm so quickly that Thea recoiled before she caught herself. "That's why you've doubted me all these years? Because of that window?"

Thea was the one who flinched. "I doubted you because you pushed me away. Because you acted as if you couldn't stand the sight of me. Because you would never let me talk about Maya."

Reggie's grasp tightened around Thea's arm. Her eyes flared a split second before the anger drained out of her and she fell back against the pillows. "That my own daughter could think that of me."

Thea rubbed her arm. "I'm sorry. I was just a kid. I didn't know what to think."

"It's not your fault. I just wish you'd come to me, is all."

"Would it have made any difference? Would you have talked to me?"

"I don't know," Reggie replied honestly. "But I'm going to tell you now what I should have explained back then. I couldn't look at you at times because you reminded me of Maya. It was just too much. I couldn't talk about her without reliving all the terrible things that went through my head every night when I closed my eyes. As for the window, I didn't mention it to the police because I didn't remember. I didn't remember because I was drunk that night. Too drunk and too high to protect my little girl. So, no, whatever you thought of me wasn't your fault. You were right to have doubts. I didn't hurt my baby, but what happened to her was every bit my fault."

The raw emotion in her voice tore at Thea's poise, but she had to hold it together. There was still too much to get through. "I believe you."

Reggie sighed. "We should have cleared the air years ago."

"Yes."

"That's my fault, too."

"I could have forced the issue," Thea said. "It was easier just to build walls."

"All that time wasted. We'll never get it back."

"We can't worry about that right now," Thea said. "I know this is hard. It is for me, too. But we need to stay focused. Kylie is still out there somewhere, and I still need to ask you some questions."

"I can't tell you what I don't know," Reggie said.

"Then we'll focus on what you do know. Was Derrick ever violent with you?"

She spoke quietly but fiercely. "He was a violent man, but he never laid a hand on me or you girls. If he'd ever so much as thought about hurting either of you, he wouldn't have lived to see the inside of a prison cell."

Thea felt a prickle of apprehension as she studied her mother's expression. There was still so much about Reggie she didn't know or understand. A few tender moments didn't change that. "Is there anyone you can think of who might have had a reason for kidnapping Maya? Someone who held a grudge against you? Or anyone you suspected at the time whether they had motive or not?"

Reggie turned her head away, as if considering the question.

"What is it?" Thea prompted. "I can tell you thought of someone."

"You have to understand, I was out of my head with worry and grief after it happened. A lot of bad things went through my mind."

"Like what?"

Reggie frowned, thinking back. "It was something June said to me after your daddy's funeral. Everyone had gone back to her house after the service. She met me on the front porch and told me I wasn't welcome. I knew she blamed me for Johnny's accident. He'd been with me earlier and we'd both been drinking. I never realized until I saw the way she looked at me that day how much she truly despised me. She told me if it took the rest of her life, she'd find a way to make me feel what she felt at that moment."

"She's hateful and vindictive," Thea said. "That's not news. But you don't seriously think she had anything to do with Maya's disappearance, do you? She certainly wouldn't have any reason for abducting Kylie Buchanan."

Reggie's head whipped around. "You think the same person took both girls?"

"They disappeared through the same window. As you noted yesterday, that can't be a coincidence." Thea paused. "You said Derrick was never violent toward you, but when I saw him in the woods earlier, he told me flat out he has a score to settle with you. Do you know why?"

Reggie shrugged. "No man likes to be rejected. Especially a guy like Derrick Sway. He always thought he was God's gift to women."

Thea didn't buy her explanation. "You'd been broken up for years when he went to prison, so I don't think rejection is a motive. Maybe he thinks you're the one who turned him in to the police. Were you?"

"If I'd turned a guy like Derrick Sway into the police, I'd know enough to keep my mouth shut about it," Reggie said.

Thea took that as a qualified yes. "Do you have any idea where he might go to hide out? Any friends you know of that he remained close to?"

"Since I don't associate with any of the old crowd, there's no way I could know that."

Thea fell silent, contemplating Reggie's responses.

"Are we done now? My painkillers are wearing off and my head is starting to hurt."

"There's just one more thing I need to ask you."

Reggie rubbed her temples. "It can't wait?"

"No. I'm sorry, it can't. I hate having to bring it up, but I need to ask about the box that was found in the woods after Maya went missing."

Reggie closed her eyes. "What about it?"

"It had Maya's DNA inside and yet all this time you still believed she was alive?"

"Of course it had her DNA," Reggie said. "Someone put her doll and blanket inside so the cops would believe I murdered my own child and buried her in the woods. That box was a prop. A way to point the finger at me."

"Are we back to June as a suspect?"

"No. As much as she hates me, I don't think she would have done anything to hurt Johnny's children."

"Hates? As in the present?"

"I've made my peace with her," Reggie said. "I can't say she's done the same."

"Do you ever see her?" Thea asked curiously.

"I stop by now and then to see how she's getting on. She never invites me in. She likes to stand on the porch looking down on me the way she did that day after Johnny's funeral."

Thea felt unexpectedly defensive of her mother. "Then why do you bother going over there?"

"Somebody has to," Reggie said with a shrug. "Her friends are dead. The neighbors have all moved away. You're the only blood kin she has left. Besides, I've come to accept her for who she is. She's too old to change. I know she must get lonely rattling around in that big house. You should go see her while you're here."

Thea bristled at the suggestion. "I'm not here to socialize."

"She's your grandmother. She has a right to see her only grandchild."

Thea could hardly believe her ears. "Are we talking about the same June Chapman who once called me an abomination?"

Reggie muttered under her breath. "I won't make excuses for her behavior."

"Good."

"But I know what it's like to lose a child. How the grief festers and spreads until you're all but consumed by the pain."

"Your circumstances were completely different," Thea argued.

"Loss is loss. Grief is grief. Go see her, Althea. Make your peace before it's too late."

"Why does it matter to you so much?"

Reggie drew a long breath. "Because I hope someday a child of yours will show me the same charity."

Chapter Twelve

Thea sat with Reggie for the rest of the afternoon, waiting for a phone call from Jake that never came. She'd known it might be morning before they heard definitive news, but as twilight fell and the dinner trays came and went, she began to grow jittery, imagining all sorts of life-threatening scenarios at the cave.

"Althea, stop that pacing! You're getting on my last nerve," Reggie complained. "Go back to your hotel and get some rest. We'll know when we know."

"Are you sure you don't want me to stay the night?"

"I'm fine. There's a cop right outside my door if I need anything. Now go. You look as if you're ready to keel over."

Thea finally relented. Reggie was safe in the hospital. Might as well go back to her room and try to get some sleep. Besides, a hot shower and some food would go a long way to boosting her morale. She said good-night to Reggie and walked outside to a full moon and a mild breeze. *Jake, call me*, she implored as she climbed into his SUV. Her phone had been smashed in the confrontation with Derrick Sway, but he knew to reach her at the hospital or her hotel.

As soon as she got back to her room, she checked for messages and then took a shower and ordered dinner. Stretching out on top of the covers, she closed her eyes. Sometime later, a knock on the door startled her awake. She straightened her robe and smoothed back her tangled hair as she got up to glance through the peephole. Not room service, after all. She opened the door and silently stood back for Jake to enter.

"I didn't expect you to show up in person," she said anxiously as she followed him into the room. "I thought you'd call if there was news. The divers—"

"Found nothing."

She closed her eyes. "Then why are you here?"

"I have other news." He seemed on edge as he turned to face her. "I tried to call you at the hospital. Reggie answered. She recognized my voice when I asked for you. I'm sorry, but I couldn't hold off. I had to tell her."

Thea's heart thumped painfully. "Tell her what?"

"It's not Maya."

Thea let out a harsh breath and dropped to the edge of the bed. "You know for certain? I didn't expect a definitive answer until tomorrow."

"Yes, we're certain. The skeletal remains are that of a male Caucasian. We won't know much more than that until Dr. Forrester and her team can examine the bones in the lab." He sat on the other bed, facing her.

"What about the etching on the rock and the wind chimes in the tree?" Her hands were trembling so she clasped them together in her lap. "They weren't placed above the cavern randomly. The stick figures are too much like Maya's drawing to be a coincidence."

"Yeah, I've been wondering about that myself," he said. "My only guess is that someone else thought the remains were Maya."

Thea glanced up. "Or maybe there's another grave nearby."

He met her gaze and nodded. "I won't lie, I thought about that, too." He paused. "Are you okay?"

"Yes," she said numbly. "I'm not even sure how I feel at the moment. We've waited so long to know what happened to her. Then when we thought she'd been down in that cave all these years…that someone may have been visiting her grave for God only knows what purpose…" She shuddered. "It's not an image you want in your head."

"I'm sorry," he said again.

"So now we're back where we started." She took a moment to gather her thoughts. "Do you have any idea who he was? The man in the grave?"

"Not yet. Chief Bowden is checking the local database for any missing persons in the area that match the general description. The digital records only go back so far and then someone has to comb through the physical files. We're checking our own databases, of course, but that's also a process."

"Is it possible he got lost in the cave?" Thea asked. "Maybe he was homeless or a runaway who crawled inside to get out of the elements."

"Not likely. Dr. Forrester found several cuts on at least six bones of the rib cage, suggesting our John Doe was stabbed."

"Brutally, by the sounds of it." Thea let that sink in. "And then his killer dragged the body into the cave and buried him underneath a mound of rocks and debris."

Jake looked grim. "More than likely, the victim was lured into the cave. I don't see a body being dragged through all those narrow tunnels. You don't remember any other disappearances in the area?"

"Not that I recall, no."

"I didn't expect you would. By all indications, the remains have been down there for decades. Maybe longer than you've been alive."

"Do you think the remains could be the reason Derrick Sway has been hanging around in the area?"

Jake shrugged. "Impossible to say since we don't yet know the victim's identity."

Thea grew pensive. "It's just that Sway said something to me earlier I haven't been able to get out of my head. He said he was surprised Reggie Lamb had raised a cop because, when he knew her, she wasn't the law-and-order type. Then he asked if I remembered sleeping in the back seat of his car. When I said no, he said it was a good thing. I might have seen something that was bad for my health."

"What do you think he meant by that?"

"No idea. He was neck-deep in a lot of criminal activities back then. Maybe he talked Reggie into helping him with something illegal and she brought us along."

Jake looked skeptical. "She would do that?"

"Not the present-day Reggie, but she was a different person back then. It's possible she got in over her head with Sway. Maybe Maya woke up in the back of his car and saw something she shouldn't have. Maybe that's why she was taken instead of me."

"That's one theory. But it's just a theory."

"I know." Thea bit her lip. "I guess I've wondered for so long why my sister was taken instead of me that I'm willing to reach for any explanation."

His gaze softened. "I can understand that."

"Still, no matter how willing Reggie was to skirt the law, she would never have been party to murder, much less to hurting her own child. I'll admit, I've had my doubts over the years, but I saw her face today when she thought Maya had been found in the cave. If Sway took my sister, he either acted alone or had another accomplice. It wasn't my mother."

"Reggie's neighbor made an interesting observation about her yesterday," Jake said. "If she knew Sway had done something to Maya, she would have kept silent only if he threatened to hurt you."

Thea felt a pang in her chest at the possibility. Had she misjudged Reggie all these years? "Maybe that's why she turned him in years later for a crime unrelated to the kidnapping. She needed to find something that wouldn't blow back on her or me. But someone talked and Sway decided to retaliate by taking Kylie. Whether he thought she was my child or not, he had to know how deeply her abduction would hurt Reggie." Thea got up to pace. "We have to find him, Jake."

"We're doing everything we can."

"I know, I know. It's just…"

"The clock is ticking."

She jumped when a knock sounded at the door. Jake

glanced past her to the entranceway. "Are you expecting someone?"

"Room service."

He rose. "I'll get out of your hair and let you have a peaceful dinner."

"No, stay," Thea said impulsively. "That is, if you haven't eaten yet. It's just a burger and fries, but I don't mind sharing."

He looked doubtful. "Are you sure?"

"Yes, stay." She got up to answer the door. The young man who brought in the food laid everything out on the table by the window. Thea signed for the meal and then closed the door behind him. She sat and motioned for Jake to take the seat across from her. She divided the order and handed him a plate. He sat and dug in.

"This hits the spot," he said between bites. "I didn't take time to eat earlier. I cleaned up and came straight here."

"We can order something else if this isn't enough."

"It'll do for the moment."

Thea devoured a fry, finding herself likewise ravenous. "The neighbor you mentioned earlier. Would he happen to be Lyle Crowder?"

Jake glanced up. "Yes, why?"

"I talked to him earlier. He was looking in the windows of your Suburban when I came out of Reggie's house."

"Why the face?" Jake asked.

"Did I make a face?"

"Subtle, but yeah. You don't like him?"

"I never had anything against him personally, but he

always gave Reggie the creeps. She told me I wasn't to let him in if he ever came to the door when she wasn't home."

"But she had no problem letting someone like Derrick Sway into her house."

"It does seem a contradiction," Thea agreed. "But like I said, she changed after Maya's disappearance."

"Did she give you a reason for her distrust?"

"She said she didn't like the way Lyle stared across the street at our house. The funny thing is, he never seemed to be looking at me. I assumed he had a thing for her. A lot of men did. She was an attractive woman back in her day."

"Your mother is still an attractive woman," Jake said. "I can see a lot of her in you. Same bone structure and coloring. Same fearlessness."

Thea had gone silent.

He frowned across the table. "Did I say something wrong?"

"What? No. I was just wondering where Lyle Crowder was the night Kylie disappeared."

"He was on a fishing trip with his brother. He didn't return home until Monday afternoon."

"You've checked out his alibi?"

"Of course. Why? What are you thinking?"

"He used to work on offshore oil rigs when I was a kid. He was sometimes gone for months at a time."

"So he told me."

"He had an old bluetick coonhound with him when we talked earlier."

"Okay," Jake drawled. "I'm a little lost here. What does one have to do with the other?"

Thea felt a tingle of excitement along her backbone. "He's had that breed for as long as I can remember. He told me he left his dogs with his brother when he was working. But the night Maya went missing, we heard a hound baying in the woods."

"I doubt Lyle Crowder was the only one around here who had a coon dog."

"No, of course not, but I've had the same feeling as you that we're missing something hidden in plain sight. Could the clue that solves both cases be something as simple as a dog baying in the woods?"

Jake eyed her across the table. "It seems a stretch."

"Maybe, but just think about it. He's been living across the street the whole time, watching from the shadows of his front porch. He would have known about Reggie's party the night Maya was taken. He could have easily assumed that she and her friends would be so inebriated no one would think to check on Maya and me for hours. Twenty-eight years later, he would have seen Taryn and Reggie leave the house last Sunday morning. He could have walked across the street, removed the key from the flowerpot and let himself in the front door to unlock the bedroom window. Then all he had to do was wait for the lights to go out later that night."

She expected Jake to shoot down her theory, but instead he sat back in his chair with a contemplative frown. "He told me he used to go exploring in the cave. He even offered to go down with his dog and take a look around if we needed him to."

Thea leaned forward. "Are you sure his alibi is air-tight?"

"Worth taking another look," Jake said as he rose. "I need to make a couple of calls."

"Of course. I'll go freshen up and give you some privacy."

"I don't want to chase you out of your own room."

"You're not. We both know I have a conflict of interest in this case, and you need to be able to speak candidly."

"This won't take long."

"No worries." She went into the bathroom and closed the door. As tempting as it was to listen in, she turned on the tap and washed her face, brushed her teeth, and then pulled the hair dryer from under the sink to blow out her damp hair. Then, with nothing else to do, she used the little bottle of lotion on the vanity to moisturize her hands and sat on the edge of the tub to wait. After a good ten minutes, she got up and opened the bathroom door.

"Jake?"

She stepped through the door and glanced around. The bedroom was so silent she thought at first he must have left, but instead he'd stretched out on one of the beds and fallen asleep.

Thea started to wake him up, but then she realized how exhausted he must be to succumb so quickly. Draping a blanket over him, she left him to rest as she took care of the dinner tray and then turned out the lights. Crawling into her own bed, she lay on her back and stared up at the ceiling until the sound of Jake's breathing lulled her to sleep.

THE ROOM WAS still dark when Thea woke up. For a moment, she had that disquieting sensation of not knowing where she was or how she'd gotten there. Then she shook away the cobwebs and pushed herself up against the pillows. The window was open. She could feel a warm breeze against her skin as she kicked aside the covers.

A shadow moved out on the fire escape. She reached for her weapon as she called softly, "Jake? Is that you?"

He crawled back through the window. "Sorry. I didn't mean to wake you."

"You didn't. I rarely sleep through the night." She glanced at the clock on the nightstand. Just after midnight. "What were you doing out there?"

"Listening to the wind chimes in the courtyard across the street. You can hear them up here, by the way. You didn't imagine the sound last night."

"Good to know."

He turned back to the window, still listening to the night. "What is it with this town and wooden wind chimes?"

"According to Lyle Crowder, a local woman used to make them. People hung them in their trees for good luck. He said when the wind blew just right, you could hear them all over town."

"Interesting tradition."

"He said Reggie used to have them hanging from a tree in her backyard. I'd forgotten until now, but I think that sound is what awakened Maya. She thought someone was outside our room. I told her not to be a fraidy-cat." Thea sighed. "That was the last thing I ever said to my sister."

Jake turned and leaned against the window frame. His eyes glinted in the dark. "What happened wasn't your fault."

"I know. But if I'd called out to Reggie, maybe she would have come to see about us. Maybe she would have scared the kidnapper away."

He moved across the room and sat on her bed, draping a casual arm across her legs. "Kylie's disappearance has stirred up a lot of painful memories for you, hasn't it?"

"Yes. I can't help thinking there's something more I should be doing to find her. Something I should remember that could reveal the kidnapper."

"If this were another case, you'd tell the family members not to torture themselves. You'd say obsessing over what could or should have been done does no one any good, least of all the missing child."

"And I would know better than anyone that it's easier said than done not to dwell."

"None of this is easy. For the families or for us."

"But you wouldn't want to do anything else," Thea said.

"Would you?" There was a hushed, intimate quality to his voice in the dark.

She shivered. "I don't think either of us has a choice."

He thought about that for a moment. "Why did you move to Cold Cases after I left Washington? You were on a fast track. You had a lot of people in your corner, including me. It was only a matter of time before you would have been assigned a team."

She shrugged. "Somebody has to keep looking for those kids after the CARD team goes home."

"Even if Cold Cases is the place where careers go to stagnate and die?"

"Yes, even if," she said with conviction. "None of us do this for the glory."

He fell silent. Except for the gleam of his eyes, he was little more than a silhouette at the end of her bed. Yet Thea felt so physically attuned to him, she could almost hear the beat of his heart in the darkness.

He straightened. "I should go, let you get some rest."

"You don't have to. It's late. There's plenty of room here, and besides..." She trailed off. "This isn't a good night to be alone."

He didn't say a word, but instead rose and, ignoring the second bed, went around to lie down beside her. They weren't touching, but Thea felt closer to Jake than she had to anyone in a very long time.

After a moment he said, "Do you ever wonder what would have happened if you'd come with me to Jacksonville?"

She turned in surprise. "To my career, you mean?"

"To us."

She closed her eyes. "What's the point in wondering? You never asked me to come."

"You never asked me to stay."

She drew back. "How could I ask that of you? You'd worked so hard for so long. No one deserved that promotion more than you. Besides, when you finally told me you'd accepted the offer, you acted as if you couldn't leave town fast enough. I thought part of the attraction of the new assignment was getting away from me."

"You couldn't possibly have thought that."

Something in his voice caused her to tremble. "We'd come to a crossroads in our relationship. It was either commit more deeply or break up. Your leaving town made the decision easy for us."

"It was easy for you?" He turned to stare at her in the dark.

"You know what I mean." She scowled up at the ceiling and tried not to feel such deep regret. Tried not to think about the cold, empty apartment that waited for her back in DC. "It wasn't easy, but it was inevitable. We always said the job had to come first."

"That was a mistake," he said. "It worked for a while, but what we do can't be all that we are. It's too dark. There has to be light at the end of the tunnel." He paused. "I can't help wondering if you've found that light."

"Are you asking if there's someone in my life? No. What about you?"

His slight hesitation caused her heart to sink. "No."

"You hesitated," she accused.

"No one serious," he said. "No one who gets me the way you do."

She slid her hand down his arm and clasped his hand.

He squeezed her fingers. "I've missed this. I've missed you."

"After all this time?"

His voice deepened. "You have no idea how often I think about you."

Thea didn't know how to respond to that. She felt overwhelmed and a little unnerved.

"Am I being too honest?" He brought their linked hands to his mouth. Such a soft, sweet kiss and yet Thea felt a shudder go through her as she rolled to her side.

"I've missed you, too," she said. "I just didn't want to admit it."

"That stubborn streak." She heard a smile in his voice a split second before he threaded his fingers through her hair and kissed her deeply, stirring a longing she'd tried to bury since the day he'd left DC.

Nothing stays buried forever. Not secrets. Not longing. Not love.

Yes, love, although maybe she was still too stubborn to take her confession that far.

They kissed for the longest time and broke apart only to undress slowly, without frenzy or desperation. Just two old lovers comfortable in their familiarity. Two injured souls needing to find momentary light at the end of a very dark tunnel. But when their bodies joined, it was shockingly dynamic. Electric. Like the sizzle of two live power lines in a lightning storm. Thea could hardly catch her breath. Everywhere Jake touched turned to fire. Her neck, her breasts, the insides of her thighs. Clutching the covers, she arched into him, matching his rhythm until they collapsed against one another, gasping and quivering. Even then, Jake didn't let her go. He rolled onto his back and nestled her in the crook of his arm. She fit perfectly. As if she'd never been gone.

Chapter Thirteen

Jake was already dressed when Thea woke the next morning. "What time is it?" she asked sleepily when he came out of the bathroom.

"It's early. I need to go back to my room and grab a shower and shave before I head over to the command center." He sat on the edge of the bed. "If you meant what you said yesterday about finding something for you to do, come by later and I'll put you to work."

She rose on one elbow, squinting at the slash of sunlight streaming in through the window. "I need to go see Reggie first. I also promised her I'd visit my grandmother."

Jake quirked a brow. "I didn't think the two of you were close."

"We're practically strangers. I can't even remember the last time I saw her. She never wanted anything to do with me when I was growing up, and I don't expect anything has changed for her. But I'll make the effort because it seems important to Reggie and because, I'll admit, I'm curious."

"Do you need a lift?"

"I've arranged for a rental car. Should be here by nine or so. Hopefully, I'll have my new phone by then, too, if you need me."

He nodded. "I have a new phone, too. Same number." He reached for his keys on the nightstand before turning back to Thea. "Should we talk about what happened last night?"

She straightened the covers. "Yes, we probably should, but later. Our priorities haven't changed. There's still a missing child out there."

"A fact I don't forget even for a second." A mask dropped as he stood. He was already thinking about Kylie and about what he and his team needed to do in the coming hours to find her. "I'll keep in touch," he said briskly. Then he bent and brushed his lips against hers. "And we *will* talk," he promised.

She waited until the door closed behind him before throwing off the covers and climbing out of bed. A shower came first. She dug fresh clothes from her suitcase and quickly dressed. By the time she'd called the hospital to check on Reggie, her cell phone had arrived. She went downstairs and sat on a bench outside the hotel to familiarize herself with the new model while she waited for the rental car to be delivered.

A movement across the street caught her attention. Grace Bowden stood at the bay window in the Indigo Dollhouse, staring out. Thea waved, but the woman didn't respond. Her gaze seemed fixated on the street as if she were waiting for someone.

Curious, Thea got up and crossed the intersection.

She pecked on the window and, after a few moments, Grace opened the door.

"Thea! What are you doing here so early?" Grace looked pretty and summery in a floral dress and sandals, but there was still something about her bright smile that didn't quite ring true to Thea.

She motioned behind her to the hotel. "I was sitting outside just now and noticed you in the window. I thought I'd stop by and say hello."

Grace cast an uneasy glance toward the curb as her fingers toyed nervously with the delicate gold necklace at her throat. "That's nice of you. I didn't expect to see you again before you left."

Thea gave her a surreptitious scrutiny. "Am I interrupting something? You must be expecting a client. You said you only open on weekends these days unless you have an appointment."

"Yes, I have a collector coming in later. The meeting has the potential to be a lucrative transaction for me."

"Then why do you look so upset?" Thea asked. "Forgive me if I'm being too nosy, but I can't help wondering if something is wrong."

Grace glanced once more at the street before she stepped back and motioned Thea inside. "A woman called my house this morning." She closed the door behind them. "She said she was looking for an antique doll for her niece. I explained I had a meeting today and suggested she come in on Saturday to look at my inventory. She insisted on coming in first thing this morning. She said she's leaving the country today and won't be back for quite some time."

"Did she give you her name?"

"Valerie something-or-other. I jotted it down, but it was probably made up. I think she was calling for Russ Buchanan."

Thea frowned. "What makes you think that?"

"The woman was very specific about the doll she wanted for her niece. Her description was nearly identical to the antique doll Russ bought for Kylie's birthday."

"What did you tell her?"

"I couldn't give her an exact match. Most of my inventory is one of a kind, but I told her she was welcome to come in and take a look at my collection. When I inquired about her niece's name and age, she hung up. I know it sounds crazy, but I can't stop thinking about that call. I can't help wondering…"

"What?" Thea prompted.

"I know this sounds crazy, but do you think Russ Buchanan and that woman could be taking Kylie out of the country?"

"One phone call isn't much to go on," Thea said. "Have you told Chief Bowden about the call?"

"No, not yet. He's just so busy at the moment." She bit her lip. "You don't think I'm overreacting? The last thing I want to do is waste Nash's time or send him on a wild-goose chase."

"I think it's always better to be safe than sorry," Thea said. "Tell him what happened and let him decide how to proceed."

"You're right, of course." Grace hurried around the counter to grab her phone. "I just can't stop thinking about poor little Kylie. She was so shy and nervous the day Taryn brought her into the shop. A child deserves better than a philandering, abusive father and a mother who's so neglectful she allowed her own child to be taken right from under her nose." She glanced up, stricken. "Oh, Thea, I'm so sorry. I wasn't thinking."

"It's fine. Should I leave while you make the call?"

"Oh no, please stay. I'd rather not be alone if the woman shows up. Or, God forbid, Russ Buchanan himself. Besides, I could use the company. Go on into the kitchen and help yourself to a cup of coffee. I won't be but a minute."

Thea walked into the back and glanced around. Something was different about the space. She tried to pinpoint the change as she listened to Grace's low voice in the other room. Then she had it. The child-sized table and chairs was missing from the corner.

She glanced over her shoulder into the shop. She hadn't noticed earlier, but the shelves were even emptier than when she'd been in the day before. Was Grace clearing out her merchandise for some reason?

Taking out her phone, she called Jake. He answered on the first ring. "I was just about to call you." He sounded tense.

"What's going on?"

"I'm at the hospital with Reggie." Thea's heart jumped to her throat, but before she could respond, he said quickly, "She's okay. I wanted to talk to her about Derrick Sway."

Thea's pulse was still thumping. "Are you sure she's okay?"

"Yes, she's fine. I'm just leaving her room now."

"Was she able to tell you anything?"

"About Sway, no. But she did tell me something interesting about the Bowdens."

Thea's gaze shot into the outer room. "That's…a coincidence."

"Why?"

She turned away from the doorway and lowered her voice. "I'm with Grace now."

"At her shop?"

"Yes. She said someone called earlier looking for a doll identical to the one Russ Buchanan bought for Kylie a few months ago. She had the impression the woman was calling on Russ's behalf. The woman said she needed to buy the doll this morning because she's leaving the country and won't be back for some time."

"Where is Grace now?"

Something in his tone sent a prickle of fear up Thea's spine. "What's going on, Jake? What did Reggie tell you?"

"Don't react, just listen. Your instincts were right about the Bowden marriage. Grace and Nash Bowden were separated for a long time before they finally divorced over a year ago."

"Okay," Thea said in a neutral tone.

"Reggie said when Grace was a kid, she seemed to have an unnatural obsession with Maya's disappearance. She was always asking questions about her, always wanting to see pictures of her. Reggie would sometimes catch her in your room going through the dresser drawers and closet while you were outside playing. She put up with the behavior for a while because no one else was allowed to come to the house and play with you. Then things went missing. She eventually told Grace not to come over anymore."

"I don't get why this is important," Thea whispered into the phone.

"Five years ago, Grace lost a baby. She never got over it. The child, a girl, would have been the same age as Kylie. Grace has intimate knowledge of Reggie's house and Maya's disappearance. And she misled you about the state of her marriage. It's not proof of anything, but it's enough to make her a person of interest."

"I see." Thea's gaze flicked around the space while they talked. The back door opened to the patio and a second door led to, presumably, a storage area. The building was ancient. There might even be a cellar with walls thick enough to drown out a child's cry for help.

"Thea, are you there?"

"Yes."

"Keep her talking if you can, but be careful what you say to her. She may be volatile and possibly dangerous. I'm on my way to the shop now."

"Okay." Something had come back to Thea as she fixated on that closed door. She could almost hear Reggie's voice in her ear.

That girl is a thief and a liar, Althea. A bad seed if I ever saw one. I don't want you hanging around with her anymore. Every time she comes over, something turns up missing. Hairpins, books, a picture from my dresser. I'll bet you anything she's the one who took my wind chimes.

The memory was so vivid that for a dangerous moment, Thea became lost in the past. Jake's voice in her ear and the creak of a floorboard startled her back to the present. She whirled a split second before the Taser barbs connected with her skin and every muscle in her body started to spasm.

THEA DIDN'T REMEMBER losing consciousness, but she must have. When she opened her eyes, she found herself on the floor in a strange room, one hand cuffed to an old iron bedstead. The blast from the Taser wouldn't have incapacitated her for more than a few seconds. Long enough to drag her outside and heft her into the back of an SUV? Then what?

As her mind cleared, the images came back stronger, along with the hazier sensation of a needle prick in her arm.

She straightened on the floor and jerked at the handcuffs as she craned her neck to glance out the window. The landscape was wooded, and she could see the gleam of a lake in the distance. They were no longer at the doll shop. No telling how many miles they'd traveled from Black Creek while she'd been unconscious. She had no idea how long she'd been out, but judging by the brightness of the sun, no more than a few hours. It was still broad daylight outside.

She tried to quell the roiling in her stomach as she took stock of her surroundings. The room was sparsely furnished with a bed, dresser, nightstand and lamp. Nothing within her limited reach that could be used for a weapon or lockpick.

Directly across from her was an open closet. Inside

the shadowy recess, a child hunkered with her head buried against her knees and her arms clasped around her legs. She was so still and silent that, for a moment, Thea thought she might be sleeping.

"Kylie?" She said the name so softly the child didn't appear to hear her. "Kylie Buchanan, is that you?"

The child kept her face buried as she tried to push herself deeper into the closet.

"It's okay, sweetheart. I'm not going to hurt you. I want to take you home to your mommy."

Still no sound or reaction.

"Do you know Reggie?"

The head finally bobbed up.

"I know she's a friend of yours. I'm her daughter, Thea."

Kylie dropped her arms from around her legs and scooted to the edge of the closet, poking her head out to survey the room before she scrambled to her feet.

"Is my mommy dead?"

Her quivering voice tore at Thea's heart. "No, honey, she's not dead. She's worried sick about you, though. She misses you very much."

The child inched closer. "She said Mommy died. She said my daddy killed her."

Thea tamped down the horrified gasp that rose to her throat. "Your mommy is fine, I promise."

"Will you take me to her?"

"Yes, just as soon as I can. I may need your help, though, okay?"

A reluctant nod.

"Do you know where we are?"

She shook her head.

"Are you okay? Have you been hurt?"

Another headshake. "I want my mommy."

"I know, sweetie, I know. I need you to do something for me. Go back into the closet and see if you can find something sharp, like a safety pin or a belt buckle. Anything metal. Can you do that for me?"

The little girl went back over to the closet and dropped to her knees to explore. A few minutes later, she crawled back out with something clutched in her fist. She approached Thea shyly and held out her hand, displaying a child's hairpin adorned with a pink plastic flower.

"Is this yours?" Thea asked, then froze in recognition. She and Maya had had nearly identical hairpins. Thea's had been yellow. This one was pink. "Is there anything else like this in the closet?"

Kylie shook her head.

Thea stared at the pink plastic rose. Had Grace taken the keepsake when she was a child or had she entered Reggie's house more recently to unlock the bedroom window?

She glanced back outside. Where were they? Surely not at Grace's home. She wouldn't take the chance on hiding Kylie where she might be spotted by neighbors. No, they were someplace remote, but close enough to town that Grace could easily drive back and forth while she made arrangements.

A car pulled into the driveway just then. At the sound of the engine, Kylie dashed across the room and scooted back into the closet. A few minutes later, a door closed in the outer part of the house. Thea slipped the hairpin underneath the mattress and lifted a finger to her lips as her gaze met Kylie's. A split second later, the bedroom door opened and Grace Bowden stepped inside.

"I didn't expect you to be awake so soon. I thought you'd be out until after we left. Not that it matters all that much. Everything is still going according to plan."

"What plan is that?" Thea asked. "Where are you taking her?"

"Somewhere safe for both of us." She glanced around the room. "Come out, dearest. Don't be shy. I've brought your favorite lunch. It's waiting for you on the table along with a little surprise. Come on, now. Don't you want to see what I've brought you for our trip?"

Kylie stared out from the back of the closet with wide, frightened eyes.

"It's okay," Thea coaxed. "Go eat your lunch. I need to talk to Grace."

"Don't tell her what to do," Grace snapped. "You're not her mother."

"Neither are you."

"Don't listen to her," Grace said to Kylie. "I am your mommy now. I'll take such good care of you. You'll love where we're going. It's warm and sunny, and we can swim every day if we want to. Please come out and eat your lunch. We need to get on the road soon."

Thea caught Kylie's eye and nodded. The child crawled out and reluctantly followed Grace into the other room. Thea could hear a TV or radio from another part of the house. A few minutes later, Grace came back into the bedroom and closed the door. "I know you must have questions. Not that I owe you any explanations, but I always liked you."

Thea stared up at her. "Yes, I have questions. Why are you doing this? You know you won't get away with it."

Grace smiled. "You might be surprised. People have always underestimated me. As to the why…it's very simple. Every child deserves a mother who will love and protect her unconditionally."

"Kylie has a mother who loves her."

"But she couldn't protect her, could she? Not even from the child's own father." She knelt, putting them at eye level but keeping her distance. When Thea shifted away from her, Grace said, "Oh, don't worry. I've no intention of hurting you. We were friends once. I always thought we could have been best friends if Reggie hadn't been so mean to me."

"You stole things from our house," Thea said. "She didn't like that."

"She had no proof that I took anything."

"But you did, didn't you? You took her wind chimes and hung them from a tree over an opening that led into the cave. How did you even know the opening was there?"

"I stumbled across it one day. My parents didn't care what I did so long as I stayed out of their way. My aunt Lillian meant well, but she was clueless when it came to precocious children. Sometimes when I got lonely or felt sorry for myself, I'd spend hours in the cave exploring. That's how I found Maya's grave. I hung Reggie's wind chimes in the tree to keep her company."

"And the stick figures etched into the rock?"

Grace shrugged. "She needed a headstone and I knew she'd want you close."

"You saw her drawing on our refrigerator. That's where you got the idea for the stick figures."

"I always loved that drawing. You and Maya holding hands for all eternity. I used to wonder what it would be like to have a sister. To have *someone*."

"Why didn't you tell anyone about the grave?" Thea asked. "If you truly considered me a friend, you would have told me."

"I wanted to," Grace said. "But I liked having a secret too much."

"It made you feel special. Important...?"

"Yes," she admitted candidly. "Oh, I fully intended to tell you someday. I imagined how I would do it all the time. I'd lure you into the cave and lead you back to the cavern. You'd be awestruck when you realized what I'd found. But you were always such a fraidy-cat. You wouldn't even climb over the fence, much less go down into the cave with me. Then, after Reggie told me I couldn't come over anymore, I didn't want you to know. I didn't want her to know."

"You decided to keep Maya all to yourself. Except it isn't Maya in that grave."

Grace looked momentarily surprised before she shrugged. "It was still a good secret."

"When did you decide to take Kylie?"

"I'd noticed her for years. Sometimes when Taryn would take her to the park, I'd close the shop early and walk down the street so that I could watch them through the fence. She's such a lovely child, with a sweet, shy disposition. After a while, it became painfully obvious how desperately unhappy she was. It wasn't fair that she should have to suffer or that I should be so lonely when the two of us could have each other.

"When I heard that she and Taryn were staying with Reggie, I started to make plans. Even then, I wasn't sure I could go through with them. Then that night—Sunday night—I drove back to the church after the service just to catch another glimpse of her. I saw Taryn get out of her vehicle and go into the building without Kylie. She left her alone in the car after dark. Anything could have happened to that child. I knew then it was up to me to protect her."

"So you took her. You planted Maya's picture in Derrick Sway's bedroom and you hung those totems in the woods so that everyone would assume he'd kidnapped both Kylie and Maya. Then you told him that Reggie was the one who'd turned him in to the police, knowing he'd come after her."

Grace sighed. "People are predictable, for the most part. The plan worked perfectly until you showed up. But I knew eventually you'd remember how I tried to get you to go into the cave with me. You'd remember my curiosity about Maya's disappearance and the keepsakes that went missing from your house. You'd get just suspicious enough to start asking uncomfortable questions, so I needed to throw you off the scent until Kylie and I were safely out of the country."

"You drugged me that first night," Thea said. "How were you able to get into my room?"

"Security is nonexistent in that old hotel and people are trusting in a small town. I've watched that place for years from across the street. They all have their routines. It was easy to get your room number from the front desk and grab a key card from housekeeping. A little ketamine on a piece of glass and you wouldn't feel quite yourself for days."

"You won't get away with this," Thea said again. "I was on the phone with the FBI when you attacked me. They're probably already tearing your shop and home apart. It's only a matter of time before they figure out where we are."

"No one knows about this place. Not even Nash. My aunt inherited the cabin years ago and never changed the name on the deed."

"The FBI will find it, trust me."

"Eventually, but by then it'll be too late. Kylie and I will be far, far away."

"You're delusional," Thea said.

"I'm what my parents made me." She gave Thea a sad smile as she rose and moved to the door. "It's a shame, really. We could have been such good friends."

THEA WAITED TO make sure Grace wasn't coming back into the room before fishing the hairpin from beneath the mattress. Popping the plastic flower from the clip, she bent the wire to make a short L shape. Placing the long end of the L inside the handcuff lock, she turned it like a key, rotating the pin to push down the inside ridges. She had to stop more than once to quell her impatience so as not to break the thin wire. As she worked, she could hear the front door opening and closing as Grace made several trips from the cabin to the car and back. Thea had no idea of their immediate destination. Probably to the coast to board a ship somewhere. If Grace had somehow acquired passports so that they could leave the country, Kylie might never be found.

When the lock clicked open, she could have wept with relief. She flung off the cuff and stood to glance out the window. The SUV was still in the driveway. Grace was busily arranging suitcases in the cargo area.

Thea left the bedroom quickly, taking a quick survey of the living area. Kylie lay curled on the sofa with her head turned toward the TV. She seemed so absorbed in the cartoon that she didn't notice Thea when she tiptoed into the room. She didn't even react when Thea whispered her name. Then Thea realized that the child had been drugged to keep her docile for the trip.

She scooped Kylie up into her arms, nestling the child's head against her shoulder as she moved to the back of the house, searching for another way out. All the while, she expected to hear Grace burst through the front door at any moment. Hurrying through the small kitchen, Thea fumbled with the back door lock for an impossibly long time before they were finally outside. She held Kylie close as she sprinted for the trees. A shot sounded behind her and then another. She dove for cover, turning so that her body protected the child's.

"I don't want to hurt you, Thea, but I will if I have to!"

She lay Kylie gently on the ground. The child roused and whimpered.

"Shush. It'll be okay," Thea soothed.

"You can't outrun me," Grace warned. "I know these woods like the back of my hand."

Thea hunkered behind the tree and waited. After a moment, Grace grew impatient and strode into the trees. Thea braced herself, willing Kylie to silence as she waited. Grace came into view, but still Thea waited until the distant sound of a car engine captured Grace's attention. Thea sprinted forward, lowering her shoulders and crashing into Grace with enough force to take them both down. They landed hard on the ground, momentarily dazed before they each scrambled for the weapon.

The car engine drew closer as they fought. Doors slammed. Voices sounded from the back of the cabin. Thea tried to tune out the distraction as she focused on the struggle. Grace was a lot stronger than she looked, and she fought like a cornered animal, kicking, scratching and then landing a punch that sent Thea sprawling backward. Grace grabbed the gun and rolled, taking aim a split second before someone kicked the weapon from her hand and ordered her to lie facedown on the ground. Then Chief Bowden knelt and cuffed his ex-wife.

"You okay?" Jake put out a hand as Thea scrambled to her feet.

"How did you find us?"

"We're the FBI, remember?" He glanced around. "Kylie…?"

"She's over there." They both rushed to the child's side and Jake lifted her tenderly in his arms.

Chapter Fourteen

A little while later, they were back at the hospital, standing outside Taryn's room. Kylie had been examined as soon as they'd brought her in and then she'd been taken straight up to her mother. The reunion brought tears to Thea's eyes.

"This never gets old," Jake said. "This is what we live for."

"Yes, but it's not an entirely happy ending," Thea said. She moved away from the door. "I'm worried about Russ Buchanan. He won't give up his family without a fight. I'm afraid Taryn is in for a rough time if he sues for sole custody."

"She may have some leverage," Jake said. "One of his former clients swears he was hired by Buchanan to harass Reggie. We think he's the one who ran her car off the road. His testimony will give Taryn some ammunition in a custody fight."

"I hope so. After everything she and Kylie have been through, they deserve a little peace."

They moved down the hallway toward the elevators.

"Buy you a cup of bad coffee?" Jake asked.

"Thanks, but I'm on my way to see Reggie. Rain check?"

"I'll be heading back to Jacksonville in a couple of hours. Our work here is done." He punched the down arrow button. "What about you? When will you go back to DC?"

"I'm not sure. Reggie will need some help when she gets out of here. I thought I'd stick around for a few days."

"Maybe I can drive down on the weekend," Jake said. "We haven't had our talk yet. Or better yet, come see me in Jacksonville. I'll show you around the office. Let you get the lay of the land."

She frowned. "Why do I need to get the lay of the land?"

"There's an opening on my team. I'd like you to come work with me again."

"I don't know, Jake. That's a generous offer, but I've got my own work. What I do is important, too."

"I know it is. I don't see any reason you can't do both." The elevator door opened. He ignored it. "I left once without asking you to come with me. I'm not about to make that mistake again. Just think about it, okay?"

The door slid closed. Neither of them reached for the button.

Thea drew a deep breath. "Did you mean what you said? I could do both jobs?"

"Yes. I wouldn't want it any other way."

"Then I don't have to think about it. This may surprise you, but I've been considering a move for quite some time."

"You always manage to surprise me," he said.

"I have a lot of unfinished business down here. I never would have admitted this before, but I'd like to be closer to my mother."

"You both deserve a second chance."

"Yes, but Reggie isn't my only unfinished business. I need to find out what happened to my sister and to somehow make peace with my grandmother." She slipped her hand in his. "And then there's you, Jake."

The tender gleam in his eyes was like the light at the end of a very dark tunnel.

* * * * *

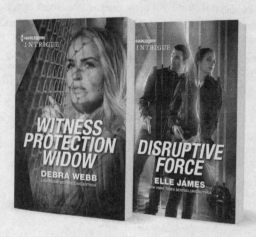

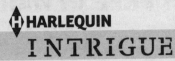

Get 4 FREE REWARDS!

We'll send you 2 FREE Books plus 2 FREE Mystery Gifts.

Harlequin Intrigue books are action-packed stories that will keep you on the edge of your seat. Solve the crime and deliver justice at all costs.

FREE Value Over $20

YES! Please send me 2 FREE Harlequin Intrigue novels and my 2 FREE gifts (gifts are worth about $10 retail). After receiving them, if I don't wish to receive any more books, I can return the shipping statement marked "cancel." If I don't cancel, I will receive 6 brand-new novels every month and be billed just $4.99 each for the regular-print edition or $5.99 each for the larger-print edition in the U.S., or $5.74 each for the regular-print edition or $6.49 each for the larger-print edition in Canada. That's a savings of at least 12% off the cover price! It's quite a bargain! Shipping and handling is just 50¢ per book in the U.S. and $1.25 per book in Canada.* I understand that accepting the 2 free books and gifts places me under no obligation to buy anything. I can always return a shipment and cancel at any time. The free books and gifts are mine to keep no matter what I decide.

Choose one:
☐ **Harlequin Intrigue Regular-Print** (182/382 HDN GNXC)

☐ **Harlequin Intrigue Larger-Print** (199/399 HDN GNXC)

Name (please print)

Address   Apt. #

City   State/Province   Zip/Postal Code

Email: Please check this box ☐ if you would like to receive newsletters and promotional emails from Harlequin Enterprises ULC and its affiliates. You can unsubscribe anytime.

Mail to the **Harlequin Reader Service**:
IN U.S.A.: P.O. Box 1341, Buffalo, NY 14240-8531
IN CANADA: P.O. Box 603, Fort Erie, Ontario L2A 5X3

Want to try 2 free books from another series! Call 1-800-873-8635 or visit www.ReaderService.com.
